PRIZE
Lilly K. Cee

Turbulent Press, LLC

Copyright © 2023 by Lilly K. Cee.

This story is a work of fiction that contains interwoven descriptions of actual events, experiences, and impressions in the author's life: truth wrapped in fiction. Again, this is a fictional story with doses of truth. Beyond that, any resemblance to persons living or dead, or localities, is coincidental.

Lilly K. Cee reserves the moral right to be identified as the author of this work.

All rights reserved. No portion of this book may be reproduced in any form or by any electronic or mechanical means, including information storage and retrieval systems, without written permission from the publisher or author, except for the use of brief quotations in a book review, or except as permitted by U.S. copyright law. In other words, don't pirate this work. If you do, may you forever be stepping on tacks and experience continuous explosive diarrhea. Artifical Intelligence (AI) was not used in the writing or design of this book. No part of this book is to be used in any connection with AI.

Developmental Review by Jeanine Harrell at Indie Edits with Jeanine

Line, Content Edits and Proofreading by Beth at VB Edits

Cover design by Lilly K. Cee/Turbulent Press LLC. Image © luda311, used under extended license from depositphotos.com. Interior image designed by Lilly K. Cee/Turbulent Press LLC

U.S. Library of Congress Control Number: Available Upon Request from Turbulent Press LLC

Contents

Foreword	VI
Dedication	VII
My Prize	VIII
Final Warning	IX
PROLOGUE	1
1. ISLAND	4
2. PRIZE	7
3. PET	14
4. A PRIZE	25
5. SHARE	31
6. DENIAL	43
7. COLLAR	51
8. NORMALIZING	56
9. VALUE	59
10. REPRESSION	63
11. BREAK	68
12. TRANSFERENCE	73

13. LIAR	77
14. MANIPULATION	81
15. FUCKING	86
16. BOUNDARIES	92
17. WHORE	100
18. DISSOCIATION	105
19. GAUNTLET	108
20. FAWN	116
21. NARLINA	122
22. KITTY, KITTY	132
23. PUNISHMENT	139
24. ATTACHMENT	145
25. CONSEQUENCES	148
26. VIGILANCE	154
27. TRUTHS	163
28. AFFECTION	168
29. SUBMISSION	173
30. REVICTIMIZATION	181
31. FLIPPED	186
32. MASKING	193
33. FIRE	196
34. FIGHT	205

35. DOLL	214
36. FREEZE	216
37. FLIGHT	220
EPILOGUE	227
Afterword	230
Acknowledgments	232
Also by Lilly…	235
About the Author	240

Foreword

<u>Author's warning</u>: This is not a romance like you're accustomed to, but I can find romance in any situation. As horrific as it is, so does our Prize. Is there a HEA/HFN? Yes, my kind of HEA. This is not dystopian, although it would make some comfortable to consider it as such. It is a nightmare set in the contemporary world, and it contains the following content and trigger warnings: Assault, Blood, Child abuse *on page* (in flashbacks), Grooming, Human Trafficking including references to BIPOC and children being trafficked, Murder, Nonconsent, Perversions of Kinks (do <u>*not*</u> follow the tenets of a consensual BDSM relationship), Profanity, Rape / Sexual Assault *on page,* Revenge killing, Reference to dog fighting (no active animal cruelty), References to child sexual assault, References to suicide/suicidal ideation, Sexually explicit scenes. The themes of revisiting childhood trauma while the main female character experiences current trauma may be distressing to some.

Dedication

To the ones who are still silent:
You don't owe anyone a justification for your pain.
Fuck 'em if they make you feel like you do.
That's their lack of empathy, not yours.
So scream.

"They broke my heart, they killed me, but I did not die."
~Sinead O'Connor

Being told your experiences weren't what you know them to have been is intended to make you powerless.

It makes you an accomplice.

But my voice mattered.

My voice *matters*.

Silent no more.

This is my Prize.

Final Warning

If you choose to proceed, welcome to the island.

PROLOGUE

Wes

Wes flicked his gaze toward Rogan and Narlina. The two were tangled together, whispering and cuddling in their after-fuck bliss. He took in the scene he'd witnessed, and had protected, since Narlina had been married off: their immediate passion and their need for one another, followed by whispered pleas and promises.

Like following a script, Narlina pleaded with Rogan, "Promise me." Desperation bled into her words. It was as palpable as the waves crashing on the shore, echoing beneath the boardwalk under which they hid.

"I promise," came the response, even if it was automatic by now.

Rogan wouldn't deny her. He wasn't capable of denying her any more than he could deny himself. She was his heart. Wes had heard the sentiment since childhood. But he wasn't confident whether her petition was for a getaway, or whether it was a form of reassurance, one that reinforced Rogan's devotion to her.

The liaison was dangerous for all three of them. Narlina's marriage to Alan put these trysts in forbidden territory. Normally, there were no restrictions regarding how people fucked on this island, but Narlina was different. She'd been chosen and groomed from a young age specifically for Alan.

Alan had been the man in charge for as long as he could remember. Though he didn't own the island. Wes and Rogan were beginning to believe the island was, in fact, corporate-owned. Too many times, they'd overheard comments referencing board approval. Alan was assisted by Larry and Trent, the accountant and logistics officer. Wes worked directly for Trent. He worked in procurement and was responsible for bringing in the flesh that fed fantasies.

It wasn't until his time on the mainland, when he'd hung around colleges and sat in business classes, that he picked up on the corporate structure. It made sense, though; this was a huge operation with a lot of moving parts.

This particular enclave had been in operation since the early '80s. Comparatively speaking, it was still in its infancy. So far, they were good at hiding. The endeavor was small enough to avoid drawing attention, though expansive enough to require its own tiny village of support staff. Rogan being one. He worked in communications, providing signal jamming, monitoring, and hacking. It was a sophisticated process that required staying one step ahead of the ever-changing and advancing tech. Information wasn't allowed in or out, but that was part of Rogan's difficult task.

When Wes was a child, Alan had appeared larger than life, even though he wasn't physically impressive. His position, power, and aura were terrifying. He could be cold and cruel with his glances and judgments, so those working on the island, and the children residing there, went out of their way to please him, to keep him happy. Rogan's continued need to fuck the man's bride was dangerous.

On the other hand, when Alan was generous, he could be likened to a favored uncle bestowing his love, and each act of benevolence was inhaled like a fresh breeze.

Rogan and Narlina were relying on that generosity. It allowed Rogan to dream of running away. They'd made a pact. When the time came for his service to the island to be rewarded, Rogan would buy his way off this volcanic rock. He had contacts and meager funds stashed on the mainland, secured in a gym locker. It was their secret, Wes's and Rogan's, that place and the combination.

It was madness, their plan, but Wes would play his part dutifully. Not for Narlina, but for Rogan. His friend had always had a soft spot for her, but Wes had never been impressed, even as kids. Narlina was too whiny, too clingy, and far too manipulative of Rogan's feelings.

Case in point: all three of them risked their lives regularly so she could have her cake and eat it, too. As a communications officer, Rogan knew where the cameras were. He knew how to bypass them, disable them, and erase evidence. But it wasn't foolproof. And while they were fucking, they were vulnerable. *Rogan* was vulnerable. That's where Wes came in. He wouldn't let anything happen to his lovesick friend.

Wes glanced over at them again. The sand wasn't a concern as they pressed their naked bodies to one another. Was he jealous? Maybe a little, though not of Rogan's relationship with Narlina. He didn't crave Narlina's affection. His jealousy stemmed from not having his own dangerous liaison. He was the faithful lookout, the foil. He would be the one left behind, scratching his head and feigning ignorance when his best friend snuck Narlina off the island.

"I promise."

Rogan hadn't needed to say it twice. They all knew where his devotion lay.

1

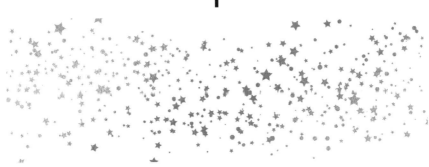

ISLAND

Rogan

People fuck. That isn't a provocative statement, it's a fact. How they fuck, who and what, can be galling, but there's big business in catering to the depraved whims of entitled rich assholes—and bitches—whose sexual proclivities are illegal. The more perverse, twisted, and cruel, the more desired it is. That shouldn't be a surprise to anyone.

The existence of private islands to accommodate these perversions also shouldn't be a shock. Its privatization allowed for the elite to exorcise their twisted fantasies. It provided a hidden and protected playpen for those who could afford it—and those whose exploitation would be devastation if their "vacations" were made public.

Fucking was celebrated. Urges were unchecked. Anything a man wanted to do to satisfy his dick was allowed, encouraged, and exploited. Women, too. They were fewer in number on the island, but their perversions matched—and sometimes exceeded—that of their male counterparts.

Indoctrination began at birth. At an early age, he'd become desensitized to the scores of men, women, and children brought in to fulfill fantasies.

For as long as he could remember, he'd understood that he, Wes, Narlina, and several other kids were treated differently. They weren't used in the same manner that they sometimes witnessed. It took years, though, to understand that most individuals used for their bodies weren't there of their own accord.

Unlike the other kids on the island, they were free to roam, to explore… everything. When he'd gotten his first boner, he'd sought out Wes. He'd shown it off, and then the two of them had spent hours getting him off. Then it was Wes's turn. Orgasms became an obsession. They beat themselves off, then each other. They'd quickly progressed to asses, then mouths. They'd been unchecked. Why would they need to be checked? Their environment informed them on the many ways to chase the pleasure, and so they did.

Then there was Alan. He would perch Narlina on his lap and touch her. Each time Rogan witnessed the interaction, he hated the man. Both Alan and Larry made his skin crawl. On instinct, Rogan steered clear. Narlina didn't have the ability to do so. But no matter how it enraged him to watch Alan pet and fawn over Narlina, there was nothing he could do. As a child, he hadn't known there was another option beyond enduring it.

If a person doesn't understand the wrongness of an action, if that concept is never introduced, then it isn't wrong. The internal compass is skewed.

Sympathy and empathy are innate. As are love and fear.

He'd had those things once, with his mother, and then Wes's mother, before they'd fucked off and left them. He had that with Narlina. And a different kind of love for Wes.

But he knew better now. He'd been to the mainland for computer and systems training, provided by others like them. Rogan worked with hackers, mostly. A few underpaid or disillusioned government workers provided passports for a handful of cash—although that was more Wes's area—affording him the opportunity to travel for the training.

While there, he was a sponge, reading books, watching their news and their movies, learning about *life*. He'd gotten hooked on a popular fast-food joint. His soul felt at peace among the crowds; he found answers to questions he hadn't known how to ask. Now, he wanted *that* life with Narlina, and he'd promised it to her.

He meant it, too. Today's ceremony would provide the cash. A sum large enough to live off rather than the measly amount he'd hidden away on the mainland. He'd buy his way off this island and sneak her with him. Their clandestine moments weren't enough. They needed more. *He* needed more. More of her, of life, of freedom.

A hand clasped his shoulder, startling him. He'd been so deep in thought, staring across the water at the distant land, that he hadn't noticed his friend approach.

"Ready?" Wes asked.

Was he? It was time to receive an award for his dedication and service to the island. Ironically, one that would take him and his love away from the very place honoring him today. This moment had been years in the making.

So, ready? Fuck yes.

2

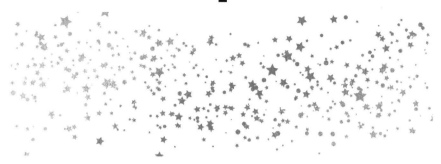

PRIZE

Rogan

The beating of his heart was the only sound. The woman, perfection sheathed in blue silk to match her blue eyes, was all he could see. Time suspended as they stared at one another. Narlina looked down at him from her perch, keeping her attention locked on him during this final moment before their world changed forever. Adrenaline jacked his heart rate higher. This was it.

A future. A life. Liberation.

In his periphery, she pushed forth a lever. As she did, her brows twitched and her lips turned down imperceptibly, her expression shifting subtly from playfulness to sorrow. Apology.

Apology?

A rumbling in the chute drew his attention, heralding the falling of a large object: the prize he'd played the long game for, the one that would buy his way off this depraved island. That would finance his and Narlina's future. The loud reverberations sent excitement coursing through his veins. A monetary prize was typically delivered in a large canvas bag; it was heavy. It could make a noise like that.

He regarded Narlina in these suspended seconds. Her blink was slow, her gaze averted. The cheers surrounding them were suddenly distorted, like he'd been transported into a fishbowl. Realization that she'd broken faith coincided with a dazzling flash of gold as the prize tumbled from the chute, rolling until it landed at his feet.

He looked down, instantly consumed by rage.

Narlina had betrayed him. The lever she'd pulled? It was the wrong one. Why? Why now? She could have chosen to stay. He would have argued, but he wouldn't have forced her to go. Her betrayal went beyond herself, of course; the act denied *him*. She'd denied him the money he needed to escape. She'd trapped him here with her—*selfish bitch*—and gifted him instead with...

A woman lay at his feet. She was pushing up on her hands, her head angled back to look up at him. Glittering gold body paint covered the entirety of her. Here was the irony; worthless gold. The source of fear in her eyes was far worse than a disorienting roll down a chute.

The crowd cheered, deeming this naked, gilded creature worthy of him and his dedication to their community. *He* saw her as a symbol of treachery, deception. Dreams set on fire.

He turned his glower to Narlina. She was clapping, a fake smile plastered on her beautiful, duplicitous face. While he'd been daydreaming of a life with her away from here, had she been planning this betrayal? Had he been relentless in meeting—and exceeding—his goals for nothing?

And this *thing* at his feet? Had Narlina picked this woman out for him? To console him?

He looked back down. She was trembling, scanning the boisterous crowd. Instinct or stupidity had her cowering, inching closer to him, as though he would protect her.

Her faith was misplaced.

The crowd took up a chant of his name. "Ro-gun, Ro-gun." They wanted his reaction, evidence that his pleasure mirrored their own. Because, of course, they would think that he had manifested this woman.

Putting his boot to her hip, he roughly flipped her.

She gasped. The power and control of his kick forced her to land on her back. Wide, wild brown eyes stared up at him. Her lips parted as she borrowed oxygen at an increased rate.

Crouching down, he pretended to assess her, appraise her, evaluate her worth. It was a farce, this show. When he palmed her breast, thumbing over her hard nipple—likely due to the adrenaline—it was to please the onlookers. To hurt Narlina. So he took his time, driving the crowd wild.

She trembled even more, her staccato breaths audible. She shrank back, so he gripped harder, a silent message that further protest would lead to more pain. She froze. Fuck her. He didn't care about her, her fears, this tainted reward.

He accepted her, because this was all he'd walk away with. He could reject her. If he did, they would kill her. Not that he cared. But then he'd walk away with nothing. If he rejected this woman, Narlina would have won on all sides: Him, here. Him, without a woman. Him, hers again.

Fuck that. He'd never be hers again. If he could see beyond his anger, he might wonder at how quickly he turned his heart against her. Then again, she'd had no problem gutting him in one instant.

He stood, jerking the goldenrod woman up as he did so. Before she could find her balance, he tossed her over his shoulder. Her naked flesh met his, the gold flecks in the paint irritating his skin, and slapped her ass, eliciting a startled yelp from her.

The spectators loved the display, most likely imagining what he'd do to her. What they'd do to her if the roles were reversed.

Regarding Narlina one last time, he registered her pale face. Her lower lip trembled even as she committed to the fake smile. Behind the mask, she was struggling to maintain. She was hurt.

Good. She was suffering the consequences of her actions.

If he could fuck this chick in front of them all, shredding Narlina's heart the way she'd done his, he would. But that wasn't allowed at this show; fucking weird rule to have on an island designed to cater to sexual depravities. So he nodded curtly, indicating gratitude and acceptance, following the script by acknowledging the generosity of Alan and his lovely, deceiving lady.

He turned and left with his prize.

• • • ● • ● • • •

Rogan unceremoniously dumped her in the corner of his apartment on an unused dog bed. His dog had died months ago. The dog had been a prize for his father. When his father died, Rogan took the dog, Ruff. His dad hadn't been imaginative.

Regardless, Rogan had loved the dog. After Ruff was gone, he hadn't been able to bring himself to remove the bed. He hadn't seen a point in it, considering he hadn't planned on remaining on the island much longer. Besides, its presence fueled his fantasies of getting a dog once he and Narlina were settled somewhere far from here.

Good enough, now, for his prize girl.

His place was small. All the housing for single adults was identical throughout the island; single men, rather. Single women weren't typical, and they were never allowed to be on their own.

The result was a building of eight-hundred-square-foot spaces with a front room, open kitchen, and a small hallway leading to a bedroom and the bathroom. His one window afforded a view of the decorated concrete wall that encased the complex and separated them from the luxurious bungalows beyond. His portion of the wall was painted with flowers and sunshine. Every year, the free children repainted the surfaces to freshen up the sun-faded images.

He hadn't thought he'd be around for the next painting celebration.

He didn't want to be around for it.

Rogan removed a beer from his refrigerator. Alcohol was regulated for the residents, but he was an asset to the island and therefore was allowed more contraband than most. He opened it and leaned back against the counter. Taking a long draw, he assessed the body of glittering gold. Her eyes were on him; her trembling hadn't abated.

As he pulled the bottle away from his lips, she opened her mouth as though to speak.

He held up his free hand to stop her. "I don't want to hear your voice. You don't get to speak. You don't know what you've cost me."

Maybe it wasn't fair, blaming her, but he was beyond giving a damn about being fair. His future was sitting in the corner on a dog bed. He wanted to shake her, hurt her, fuck her, empty his rage onto and into her. No one would stop him or raise an eyebrow. She was his property.

Property.

He'd never owned another human. He'd never had any desire to. It was ironic that he'd had this ownership thrust upon him at the moment he was to have left this compound, this island. Just as he'd anticipated venturing into the real world to be rid of the very depravity he was now an unwilling accomplice to.

What was he to think about the fact that this experience was handed over by the woman he was to have escaped with?

Did he think he'd be a cruel owner? No, never. He'd never thought he'd be an *owner*. But he could find no empathy within himself. She was lucky she had a bed. She was lucky he'd cleaned it after Ruff died.

He knew the world beyond the waters that surrounded them. He'd been in it, moved through it comfortably. He'd studied it for years, making the necessary arrangements. And he wanted to go there, live there, escape from the pretty island steeped in perversion. He wanted to go to where this woman had come from—where most of the unfortunate ones came from.

Again, he observed her out of the corner of his eye. She was hugging herself, knees drawn up. Her eyes were the same shade as her brown hair—what he could make of the shade beneath the gold paint. She was examining the space; her attention lingered on a smallish bookshelf containing books. It was contraband brought back with him from his various jobs off the island. Science fiction, mostly. Stories that hadn't been taken from him when he returned. He learned to stick to horror, sci-fi, and harmless fiction. It was almost comical that while living in a dystopian-like reality like this one that existed in the modern world, he was allowed dystopian fiction. Perhaps it was reverse psychology.

On longer assignments to the mainland, he'd read what he couldn't bring back. That was how he knew what had been taken from him today. It wasn't a fantasy, the goal of buying himself a way off the island. He *knew* what was out there. Even with the dysfunction of that world, it was better than this place.

When her eyes met his, she startled and dropped her gaze.

At least she knew her place.

The emotion that swamped him when he looked at her felt an awful lot like hate. He hated everything she represented. Fair or not. He'd expected to find his dreams at his feet today, and instead, she'd landed there. And at her appearance, all he'd worked for had vanished.

There would be no introspection, no moment of clarity where he realized that they had both been robbed of everything.

3

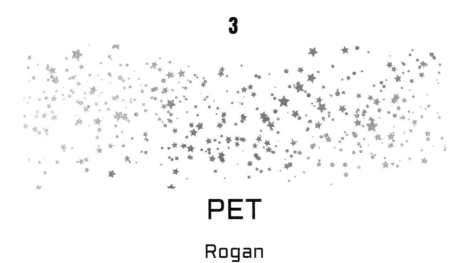

PET
Rogan

Rogan tossed her a piece of chicken, not unlike how he once tossed food to Ruff. She was sitting against the wall, eyes distant and her expression glazed over. She'd zoned out, and he couldn't blame her. There wasn't anything for her to pay attention to anyway.

He sat at the table brooding. The only reason he hadn't let his rage take over and torn his quarters apart was because he had a witness. He didn't care about her reaction or what she would have thought. He owned her thoughts; she was nothing to him. But if he'd done it, she would still have been a witness to his loss of control. A witness to how deeply Narlina had cut.

So he sat, going over every conversation and facial expression from the past year, searching for the moment Narlina had changed her mind. Considering whether she had been deceiving him the entire time, telling him what he wanted to hear. When had she begun to doubt him, their plans? Why hadn't he noticed?

Feeding himself had been a feat. Remembering to feed her more so. But he managed it.

He snapped at her. "Prize!" Because that's what she was, and she didn't deserve a name. He liked the painful reminder, the twist it gave his heart.

Of course, her presence, *his* continued presence here instead of on the mainland, ensured he didn't need a reminder.

Jerking back to reality at his bark, she whipped her head toward him. She focused only seconds before the chicken hit her on the shoulder. Looking from him to the piece of food, she timidly retrieved it; slowly, not like the starving woman she must be. She watched him for a couple of seconds before she peeled at the strip of meat and cautiously ate it.

He ignored her after that. He ate his meal and drank another beer. He pondered over the silence. Not hers, he'd demanded hers, but Narlina's. His friends'. Wes, specifically, the one person he'd trusted with his secrets, his relationship with Narlina. The one who'd swore to help them. But no one came by, no one called.

Before he'd closed his blinds, the few residents who passed by his window turned their heads away as though they didn't want to see into his apartment. Only after the third or fourth time he noticed such behavior did it dawn on him that it might be assumed he was making vigorous use of his prize. After all, he was a healthy, young, single man. But he wasn't interested in anyone but Narlina. Had he fucked other women? Of course. But Narlina was the one he wanted a future with. They'd been one lever-pull away from it. One *prize*.

Though he despised the sound of her name in his head right now, he desperately wanted to know why she'd made the decision she had. He had been mulling over reasons, searching for a way to justify it for her; maybe she had another plan in mind. A better one.

He was attempting to soothe his broken heart.

Because that look of sorrowful apology did not fit with the notion that she had alternative plans, it was an expression of plans destroyed. Her actions hadn't been made on a whim.

Shifting in the corner caught his attention. She was wiggling, grimacing, and uncomfortable. But she wasn't making a sound, and she wasn't looking up. When her hand slipped between her golden thighs and pressed, he understood her predicament. She'd been in that corner for hours.

He shoved his chair back and stood up, gaining her attention. "Come!"

She went still at his command, but only for an instant, then rose. Her steps were halting, her bare feet sounding against the concrete floor. She approached him, head down, but her eyes darted up, surveying him in small glances.

He wouldn't touch her. He didn't want to touch her; the paint was itchy. So he jerked his head. "Follow me." He strode into the hallway and stopped outside the bathroom. "Piss."

She looked into the room, something like relief passing over her face, and stepped in.

Rogan leaned against the frame and folded his arms over his chest, watching her.

Turning to take her seat, she noticed him and froze. Beneath the paint, he could detect the bright red flush. There she was: stolen, naked, and owned. He wasn't familiar with the training imposed on sex slaves—because that's what she was—and he didn't care. But she was embarrassed to pee in front of him.

"I own you, prize," he reminded her, the moniker sneering.

Her lips parted and she drew in a breath, her chest rising. She glittered with the movement. It drew his attention to her decorated breasts. Her nipples were still hard. Likely due to fear, or cold, or a combination of the two.

Either way, he didn't give a fuck.

When he dragged his focus back up to her face, she was still watching him. Her expression was full of indecision, humiliation, and a plea. Ignoring her distressed signals, he raised one eyebrow, his gaze sharply reprimanding.

Swallowing hard, the glitter making the gesture tantalizing, she slowly lowered herself onto the toilet. She gripped the sides of the seat and stared ahead, he assumed to try to ignore him. Seconds later, her bladder found relief.

And fuck him if he didn't get a small rush from the power.

He watched her pat herself dry, absorbing her humiliation as she slipped off the seat and flushed the toilet. Tilting his head, he enjoyed the red on her cheeks breaking through the gold as she washed her hands.

Cruelty wasn't normally his go-to. But today was teaching him many things.

Trailing his gaze over her, he allowed himself to note her curves. She wasn't a waif. She looked normal, other than being naked, scared, and decorated. She had a tummy, one that filled him with a compulsion to touch the softer flesh.

Narlina was thin, with very little softness to her body.

But this... What was she? Merely property? She was on Ruff's bed, so he decided to relegate her to his pet. An inconvenient stray.

She turned toward him. The trembling was back. As she tipped her chin, he looked away. He didn't want to look into her eyes. There was no reason to give her a sense of connection.

His gaze landed on his normally white toilet seat. It was covered in a sheen of gold.

With a scowl, he grasped her wrist roughly. She gasped and startled backward, but quickly caught herself. Bringing her arm up, he rubbed his other hand down her flesh and looked at his finger. Gold residue rubbed off.

"Shit." Shoving her aside, he assessed himself in the mirror. Where he'd thrown her over his shoulder, he was also marked. At least it wasn't itchy. Though if it had been, he would have been aware that she was marking everything up... namely, her bed.

Her bed. Huh.

Shaking off how quickly that notion had been assigned, he shoved her back toward the shower. She stumbled but stayed on her feet. He grasped her arm, silently signaling she was supposed to step into the tub; she did.

Reaching in, he turned on the water. When the blast hit her, she cried out. But she quickly covered her mouth to stifle the sound and turned her back to the stream. He adjusted the temperature, ignoring the startled gasping breaths she sucked in and out. Trying to, anyway.

She blinked rapidly, her expression one of distress, bewilderment, and discomfort, but she endured the cold water slowly turning warm. Popping the button on his jeans, he fought his empathetic nature. He couldn't look at her and see a human. He had to see her as his belonging. His prize, his pet. His version of Ruff.

Absolute fuckery for him to be dealing with this—a stranger he was about to shower with—on top of the devastation of the day.

He removed his boots and jeans and stepped into the tub with her, snapping the shower curtain closed as he went. She stood between him and the now warm water. Her gaze darted around. Down his naked body, quickly to the side, up at his face, and then away. The reddened hue of her cheeks under the gold heightened. She hugged herself tighter, as if still cold.

Reaching around her, their bodies meeting in the small space, his chest to her crossed arms and shoulder, he grabbed the washcloth hanging on the acrylic bar. He dangled it in front of her. "Take this."

Her dark eyes went to the cloth. She slowly reached for it.

"Wash me," he ordered. He would be easier; she was going to be a chore, as coated as she was. Gold was already streaming off her, swirling at their feet and rushing down the drain. And yet she remained tainted with it.

Her movements were timid at first, as though she was afraid to touch him. Then her brows drew together in concentration as she scrubbed him in earnest, giving him a glimpse into the task ahead of them when it was her turn. He glanced from his chest to her, studying her. For the time it took her to scrub him, he was certain she could forget her circumstances.

With a hand on his arm, she indicated he should turn. He did, allowing her to clean his back. It didn't take her as long; her body had been in contact primarily with the front of him.

A tap on his shoulder let him know she was finished. Smart girl. No words. Turning, he took the washcloth from her and indicated with a rotating finger that she should turn. He would clean her back; she could take care of her front, even if he was within his right to touch her everywhere. She was his to do whatever he wanted with, and though they'd waxed her bare, no doubt for the effect of the gold, it wasn't his preference when it came to women. His earlier inclination to fuck his rage into her had his cock twitching.

Because she was present. And her compliance was required.

She didn't have Narlina's beautiful alabaster skin, brilliant blue eyes, flowing red hair, or slender form, but his prize did have allure. The ass he was washing curved invitingly. Her breasts fit his hand perfectly, and he found the softness on her belly captivating.

Yeah, he could fuck her without a problem. He wanted to. He wanted to punish Narlina. Then again, he *didn't* want to, because he couldn't imagine sticking his dick in another woman right now. No. That was a lie. He could imagine it, he wanted it, and the conflict was pissing him off.

Narlina had *just betrayed him*. Diving into another woman wouldn't assuage the heartbreak. At the same time, he was certain it would.

Fuck.

He concentrated on scrubbing the glittery paint off her. It wasn't easy; it clung. She swayed and stumbled under his efforts, slipping in the water when he worked on the most stubborn spots. He cursed the fuckers who'd covered her in this shit. Grasping her arm, he turned her sideways.

"Hands on the wall."

She obeyed, arms outstretched, bracing herself. He worked his way down, moving to sit on the side of the tub. The curtain slipped out due to his actions, but water on the floor was the least of his worries. He scrubbed her ass, making the plumpness bounce. He squeezed a cheek; it wasn't necessary, but it'd tempted him. He considered it his reward for the manual labor he was putting in. The satisfying sound of the smack when he'd spanked her for the crowd and her answering yelp replayed in his mind.

With his face being level with...

Nope. No. He wasn't curious about her taste; the paint would taste bad, regardless. And he'd have a mouthful of glitter. What the fuck was he thinking? His mouth on her clit? Pleasuring her wasn't his job.

"Turn around," he ordered. There was no way she could scrub this all off herself, so he resigned himself to it.

She turned. The move put her pussy in his face, glinting at him. Clenching his jaw, he attacked there first, hearing her surprised gasp—and ignoring it—as the gold washed away. She flailed for purchase, her hands hovering over his shoulders, then she straightened.

Above him, her body was elongated, her breasts swaying as she clung to the shower rod. Her eyes were fixed ahead, unfocused. Not that her mental state mattered to him, he reminded himself.

As her pussy came clean of the cloying glitter, he used his fingers to spread her lips, to ensure he'd gotten what he could. That's what he told himself. Her body tensed, but he ignored her response. When he thumbed her clit, her legs jerked, and her tummy muscles contracted. Sensitive. Whatever they'd done to her, they hadn't damaged her.

He was hard by the time he finished. Her eyes were still purposefully sightless as he stood in front of her, scrubbing at her cheeks. Her breasts had been delightful to clean, if he was going to allow himself a moment of pleasure in the midst of this fucked-up situation; they'd slipped and slid in his hands. He'd indulged himself and slapped them, enjoying their buoyancy. Her nipples had hardened under his rough treatment. Did she like it rough, or was it fear?

He imagined all the ways he could use her to destroy Narlina; thus, his erection.

But he wasn't going to fuck her.

Tossing the ruined washcloth aside, he ordered her to wash her hair. That, she could manage on her own. Thanks to the electric water heater, their skin was pruned, but they were still warm. There were no natural gas pipelines leading to the island, so electricity via solar energy and petrol-powered generators kept the lights on, the water warm, and the spaces cool.

He stepped out of the tub and wrapped a towel around his waist and hard-on, then left to find clothes.

He returned with a t-shirt for her, assessing her progress. She was drying off. The shit was out of her hair, but he swore he still saw a sparkle or two. When her body was dry, he pulled the white shirt over her head. Her dark hair dampened the material. She didn't seem to notice. Nor did she try to run her fingers through her locks in an attempt to untangle it, as any girl he knew would. Narlina was constantly running her fingers through her hair.

No, this woman let her hair hang in disarray, as though hoping mussy, wet hair would be a deterrent. It wasn't. Her tits were big, her thighs were thick, and her ass was plump. Her face was pretty, and her lips looked—

Dammit.

"Clean up this mess."

She sagged at his order. Almost as if relieved. Maybe because she'd be out from under his scrutiny. The reaction meant she knew what her world would consist of for the duration of the task.

He left the bathroom, content to put her out of his mind with the same level of relief. Of course, how much relief was there to be had when he was nursing a broken heart? Grasping at his bare chest, he whispered, "Narlina." He wanted to cling to the anger. It was easier than the pain.

Rounding the corner to the kitchen, he stopped. His refrigerator door was open. "Wes."

His best friend straightened and looked at him over the door, wearing a mischievous grin. Pulling a can of beer from the fridge, he slammed the door shut. "Enjoying your new toy?" His gaze skated over Rogan's chest, then down to his sweatpants and bare feet. "Break her yet?"

"What the fuck happened?" Between the heat of the water and anger raging inside, he'd broken into a sweat. He wasn't in the mood to be teased.

Wes sighed, his mood shifting. He popped open the can. "Man—"

"You had to know."

His friend's expression was full of resignation and apology. "I didn't, not until the last minute. Not really."

"Not really?"

"You know Narlina, man. She was never going to leave. How didn't you know that?" Wes took a drink.

Rogan shook his head, the pain in his chest intensifying. "One lever," he said, his voice so low he almost didn't hear it himself.

Wes nodded. "By the time I realized things weren't going as planned, it was too late to get to you. Word came to load the chutes: one with the money, the other with a little boy. I knew then, because we were originally supposed to load both with money."

Rogan grimaced. "A little boy?"

Wes mirrored him and raked a hand through his hair. "Right? I thought, no way. If that's how it was going to play out, then you'd get something out of it. I picked her up a few weeks ago; I was having her trained for myself, but..." He waggled his brows. "I don't mind sharing."

Rogan stared. It explained Narlina's expression. Wes had disobeyed her orders, and she'd been caught off guard. Well, it wasn't like she could complain.

Wes glanced around. "Where is she?"

"Cleaning up."

Another grin appeared. "Pretty sweet something to sink into, isn't she?"

Rogan frowned, shaking his head. "I didn't fuck her. I've spent most of the evening cleaning that shit off her."

Wes's eyebrows shot up. "You're just now washing it off? That shit's itchy and toxic as hell."

"Then why the fuck didn't someone slap an instruction manual on her? And how the hell was I supposed to know how to get that off her easily? It was almost impossible."

Wes shrugged. "Not if you use vinegar."

Rogan ran a hand over his face, moving to the kitchen table. He didn't have any interest in talking about the prize. "Where's Narlina now? I want to see her."

"Where do you think she is? With her husband." Wes leaned his shoulder against the appliance, his expression solemn.

That was the moment his prize appeared. She slipped into the room, her dark hair still damp and unkempt; she hadn't used his absence to tidy her appearance, but why would she? Why would she want to look good for her captor? Her owner? The damp spots on her shoulders had expanded, absorbing the moisture. The tips of her nipples were visible through the nearly transparent material, but she didn't seem to care.

Her attention, as it should be, was directed at him. It was a nervous glance his way without maintaining eye contact. Just a quick check to gauge... what? His mood? His intentions?

When she took another step into the room, her attention was caught by Wes. Her chin jerked up, her eyes widened, and her body jolted as if she'd been electrocuted. Her freshly scrubbed cheeks paled, and she sucked in a small gasp.

Wes grinned, a hint of knowing suggestion in his expression, and he winked. "Hey, Doll. Miss me?"

4

A PRIZE
The Prize

She'd been the perfect mark. Wes had zeroed in on her immediately in the coffee shop. Of course, she'd noticed him, too. Tall, good-looking man with sandy blond hair and an easy manner and smile. His glances her way had been unassuming, appreciative without being creepy or threatening.

She'd tried to focus on her online class, one earbud in, one out; she wanted to be alert to her surroundings, even in a coffee shop in broad daylight. Her iced coffee was gathering condensation next to her. But she found her attention wandering to the man sitting across the shop, stealing as many glances at her as she was stealing at him.

She was pleased. Surprised. She'd captured his attention and had been filled with conflicting emotions, simultaneously wanting to please and wanting to hide. There were other girls, prettier girls, there. They were laughing loudly, boldly checking him and his friend out.

She remained quiet, determined to concentrate on her studies. He would finish his coffee, and he and his friend would leave. She'd never see him again. It was a sweet afternoon yearning, an ego boost to tuck away and call forth when she was feeling low.

So, though she was mildly disappointed when he and his friend gathered their things to leave, she was resigned; thankful, too, for the pleasant rush. His friend left; he didn't.

When he was alone, he wandered over to her, grinning, his light irises warm, bashful, and hopeful. "Hey, babe, mind if I sit?"

She hadn't minded the moniker. In fact, she'd felt girlie instead of offended. Murmured sweet nothings had always pleased her, even when they disguised a frightening nature. But her reaction was ingrained, her gratitude. The need to please in exchange for the cheap kindness. Of course, this time, she wanted to please.

He'd asked her about herself, had listened intently when she told him about her classes. He tapped her laptop, asking why she would come to the coffee shop to sit through class. She'd admitted she couldn't afford the Internet. Then she rushed to explain that she was on her own and was grateful for the opportunity to go to school at all, mostly via loans.

He hadn't appeared put off by her poverty. In fact, he'd looked impressed by her determination. Then he'd shared his story: he was a college student, too; criminal justice. He wanted to keep the world safe, a lofty goal. He'd laughed in a self-effacing manner. She'd been charmed.

He'd wanted her charmed.

Walking out of the coffee shop with him had felt normal, like they'd known each other for years. He made it easy. Made it feel natural. Then he offered her a ride.

No alarm bells went off, no inner voice chiding her, reminding her that she'd just met him. His car was a little older, the kind many college students possessed, not a shady-looking van. The handles were there, inside and out. Normal. It had all been so normal.

For a month, he courted her, wooed her. Took her to bed, enthralling her. He'd given her the first non-self-induced, consented-to orgasm of her life. In the beginning, she'd faked it. But he'd figured it out, and then her pleasure had become his goal. He was perfect. Handsome, funny, eager to please; he enjoyed cuddling with her in her crappy little studio apartment.

She was certain she could fall in love with him. She wanted to; she wanted to give herself over completely. And she dared to hope she could finally find happiness. That someone wanted her, had chosen her.

The abduction wasn't violent. It was nothing like she would have imagined, based on what she'd seen on television and in movies. There were no screams. She wasn't shoved into a trunk or grabbed off the street. She hadn't been drugged.

One minute, she was excited about a date on a yacht, and the next, Wes was tying her hands. When she finally understood what was happening, she didn't fight back. Instead, she shut down, slipping straight into survival mode. If she accepted this, acquiesced, she would come out the other side alive. Be good, be quiet, keep her head down.

He'd worn a look of triumph as he gagged her and blindfolded her. The efforts weren't necessary. She wasn't making any noise; wouldn't. But she'd spent hours pondering that look, focusing her thoughts there as a way to keep the terror and heartbreak from completely overtaking her.

It was an expression of pride. That he'd been correct about her.

No one would look for her, and he knew it. Her existence was a quiet one. Like a dandelion wisp on the wind. A thought of her may float through someone's consciousness, but it would be gone again so quickly, they might not have thought of her at all.

Now, she shivered on a dog bed in the corner of a room while her owner and her abductor drank beers at the table. They were talking low. Although she would guess they considered her as inconsequential as the pet her owner had quickly started treating her as (note: dog bed), it was clear they didn't want her to overhear details.

So she took stock of her situation. He hadn't raped her. Not yet, she supposed. There would be time for that. For him to use her in any way he saw fit. He wasn't happy to have her here; blamed her for events she hadn't been apprised of, but so far, it appeared that aggressive cruelty wasn't his go-to.

From what she'd learned while in her previous hellhole, training was to have taken months. She'd been hauled out of her cage early for him, though not because he wanted her. He'd won her. For what, she was unsure. But she was *not* what he'd expected to land at his feet.

It'd been terrifying, the experience, as had all the experiences since Wes had driven up to the dock that fateful day. She'd been washed, shaved, dipped in glue and glitter. When she'd heard the crowd, her thoughts immediately turned to one thing: sacrifice. Like the Romans or the Greeks. She was certain she'd tumble into a colosseum to face a hungry tiger or bear.

Instead, the gladiator at whose feet she'd landed had worn a look of fury and devastation. Though only for a moment, before he shuttered his expression. He'd assessed her, squeezed her breast, which had shocked her even though it shouldn't have. Cheeks heating, bemused that she had an ounce of modesty left within her, she'd pulled away; he'd squeezed harder. Her pussy had pulsed then, though she refused to acknowledge the reaction.

The crowd had eaten it up.

Next, she was certain he'd fuck her in front of everyone, then kill her.

But he'd scooped her up and slapped her on the ass, which had made her yelp—the sting had been as tantalizing as his pinch. Maybe it was because it was the first real sensation she'd felt outside of her mind-numbing terror.

Not that she wasn't petrified. Then he'd brought her here. She would ponder later on which would have been the preferred fate.

He'd fed her. It was a scrap, an afterthought, but he didn't intend to starve her.

He'd inferred her need to pee. Peeing in front of him had been embarrassing. It shouldn't have been. For the past few weeks, she'd peed in front of all sorts of men and women. She'd been fingered, fucked, and licked by strangers. Tied up and flogged. She'd had a device inserted to keep her jaw open while her mouth had been raped. Tears and snot hadn't deterred her assailant but she had been punished for the reaction. Forced to hang by her wrists for so long she lost feeling in her arms. It was cleverly devised, as well, to avoid marring or permanently damaging her limbs; it simply caused excruciating discomfort.

Simply.

Her owner's attention had been focused, a little curious. He'd enjoyed the power play, even if hesitantly, as if the scenario was new for him. As if he was surprised by the revelation of the excitement it brought him. Of course, he was just as quick to mask his response as he had been in the arena. But she was his now, so she expected him to explore his newfound interest.

And she was *his* even though Wes was at the table, talking in low tones with him, glancing her way occasionally. Each time he turned his eyes her way, she dropped hers. How, after everything, could she feel the sting of betrayal? How could she feel anything at all?

Although some would consider it cruel, she was thankful she'd been forbidden to speak. It relieved her of so much. It was a gift he didn't realize he'd given her.

She was grateful he'd bathed her, too, that the paint was gone. It had been horribly itchy. So uncomfortable she'd been tempted to peel her skin off. She'd willed herself to go numb in an attempt to distance herself from the pain.

But it wasn't her comfort that had prompted him. Her comfort was of no concern, evidenced by the way he'd blasted her with freezing water. Though the rough way he'd scrubbed her had been necessary, his actions held not an ounce of care. She could have been a cow.

Her body had affected him. As much as she'd forced herself to stare blankly into the void, she couldn't escape noticing his erection. She'd anticipated the moment he would shove her against the wall and plunge into her. He'd startled her when he'd left the bathroom with an order for her to clean up.

The t-shirt, she decided, wasn't for her, but for him, to cover the parts of her that his body reacted to. She wouldn't take it as a kindness or be thankful. She'd learned to be naked, to be paraded, to be used.

"Come on, take your shirt off. I have a daughter, you know. You're feverish. It will cool you down. You'll feel better." She'd been persuaded, feeling guilty for being a bother, even though it felt wrong, her being naked in front of a grown man. Her shirt came off anyway. His massage of her nine-year-old chest was to soothe, right? After all, he had a daughter.

She'd become a champion at dissociation at a young age. Not because Wes had used her, then broken her heart, and not from the training. Initially, the lessons had been deprivation-based. Clothes, name, food, basic necessities. Dehumanizing her. In her mind, she'd distanced herself, watching the techniques and analyzing the effect on her. She had been easily subdued because she'd already been conditioned. Though they likely took credit for her obedience and submission, it hadn't been *them* who had created her.

5

SHARE

Rogan

"You can breed her. If it were up to me, I'd prefer you didn't, but it's an option." Wes pulled his gaze from her.

Rogan grimaced. They'd been discussing money; rather, he'd been lamenting the loss of such a substantial amount.

"Your baby would go for a mint." He tilted his head toward the corner. "Before, she—"

"Stop. I don't want to know anything about her." He didn't want a past, an identity he could associate with her. For breeding, it might be good information, but he wasn't into that. "I'm not going to give away my baby." He'd never hand over his kid knowing the life it would lead here. What the fuck was he doing, having this insane conversation?

"Hers, then. It'll take more time, more babies, but you'll earn—"

"I'm not running a puppy mill." Even if he did regard her as no better than Ruff.

Wes sighed, playing with the beer bottle in front of him. "You better take her to the clinic, then, and get her fixed."

Rogan frowned. "She isn't?"

Wes shook his head. "They use condoms in training. Some people want to breed their slaves."

"I don't want a *slave*," Rogan growled, red-hot anger searing his insides. He scratched his trimmed beard, considering the merits of plummeting into the zoned-out oblivion she'd found more than once since he'd brought her here.

Wes leaned forward. "I had to make a decision. I had an hour from the time I learned the truth and the moment that lever was pulled. An hour to make this as right as I could. Nothing less than *her* would have been acceptable. Money, or her."

"You could have loaded the other chute with money, like the original plan."

"I didn't have access to it. That was Narlina's part." He shifted, glancing once more toward the corner. "But I knew I could have her prepared and brought up. Only one person side-eyed me, but no one would begrudge you getting her."

Waffling between heartbroken fury and worry that his love might be in danger while he was sitting here, useless, cursing her, he asked, "Could Alan have suspected something?" Rogan hated the thought of Narlina being in danger, and he desperately wanted to cling to any possibility that would have forced her hand in betraying him—them.

"You'd both be dead. Or worse." He glanced over again.

Worse: given over to the same fate as the woman—his pet—in the corner.

"Do you want me to take her?"

There was a hint of hopefulness in his voice. Prizes had been regifted in the past.

But he recalled the expression on Narlina's face. "No. I want her pain. I want her regret. I don't want to relieve her of any of it by giving… it to you."

"It." Wes snorted. "At least give her a name so I know what I can call her. Your dog had a name, for Christ's sake."

Rogan considered the suggestion. He'd already been calling her Prize, but maybe she'd been assigned a number or a moniker already. He turned in his seat and looked over at her. "Hey!" he snapped, studying her reaction.

She blinked, coming back from wherever the fuck she'd zoned out to, and peered over at him in question. As quickly, she dropped her gaze.

"What's your name?"

She was still averting her gaze, but from here, he could see her eyes widen.

"Rogan," Wes prompted. "You told her not to speak."

"When I ask you a direct question, you answer. But only me." He cast Wes a stern look. His friend would spend the evening chatting away with her if he didn't lay down boundaries.

When he turned back to her, she was regarding them warily, chin still dipped, eyes darting from one man to the other under her thick lashes, like it was a test, a trick.

Rogan waved a hand impatiently.

Finally, her lips parted, and she answered. "Prize."

Her voice. Jesus Christ. Low, the hint of a rasp in that one word, like cigarettes and coffee. He had a sudden vision of her in the speakeasy he'd visited on the mainland. Cast in shadow in a dimly lit room, voluptuous body sheathed in a red gown, like vintage Hollywood. It made his cock twitch.

No. It wasn't her looks or her voice that affected him that way. It was because she'd claimed what she was. She'd been smart enough to pick up on the cues. He'd been barking it at her. Thus, she recognized his authority, his ownership. She could have chosen any name: Lulu, Poppy, Veronica, 24601—Jean Valjean's prison number; he'd read it in one of his contraband books—and he would have called her that. But she'd chosen his name for her.

It wasn't supposed to get him off, but it did.

A snicker slipped out of the man across the table. "Are you sure you don't want her speaking? Fucking sexiest voice I've heard in a long time. It's part of why I wanted her. Having her read to me while I fucked her? Next level, man. And when she'd scream my name when she came?"

Turning away from her, Rogan snapped, "No." No, because it was a tempting thought. Already, her voice had bewitched him—it was seduction and sex—and she'd only said one word: Prize. A word that should infuriate him.

Hearing his own name in that siren's whisper would be his doom.

What the fuck was he thinking? She already was his doom.

Wes gave him a disappointed frown. "Can she talk when you're not around?"

Rogan stared at him. What was his friend planning? Or should he ask himself what *more* his friend was planning? And why was he suddenly jealous that Wes had heard her speak? Why did he suddenly want to own all of her sounds? Turning to her, he bit out a harsh "no."

But she wasn't looking at them. Once again, she'd zoned out. She looked ready to fall asleep, her knees drawn up, her arms wrapped around them. She'd tucked herself back into the corner.

"Prize!"

Startled, she sat up straighter, alert.

"Come here." It was time to relay the rules, shit he'd have to make up as he went, because he'd never seen himself in a position like this.

She planted her hands on either side of her and started to stand.

"No, baby doll. Crawl."

Rogan didn't react to Wes's directive; he simply watched her. She froze in a crouch. She assessed Wes. Her cheeks flushed red. Then she started to move, to obey, but quickly stopped. Her questioning gaze turned to him for confirmation. The silent plea in her wide-eyed look of supplication was blatant: *don't make me crawl.*

This morning, he wouldn't have believed himself the type of man to watch a woman associated with him be degraded. This morning, he would have told Wes to fuck off and leave her alone. But this morning, he'd had a heart in his chest instead of bitterness and ash. This morning, he hadn't owned another person.

So he pushed back against her petition for decency and his innate desire to give it. He raised one brow. "You were told to crawl." He didn't need to look to know Wes was smiling.

There was a brief flutter of her eyelashes, maybe even moisture as she batted away a tear. He didn't care. Then she went to her knees. Her gaze bounced between them.

Wes shifted in his chair, the only sound in the room the fabric of his pants on the furniture. "To me."

Rogan didn't intervene.

She hid her humiliation by dropping her head. Rogan tilted his, curious and aroused. The power he'd felt earlier in the bathroom surged again. The cruel hit was heady.

She jerked forward, but her hands and knees didn't move, like a battle waged within her; as if part of her was fighting for dignity. He held his breath, wondering if she would rebel; after all, she hadn't completed training, whatever that entailed.

He was supposed to punish her if she disobeyed, but he didn't know what that involved either. Again, she hadn't come with an instruction manual. He willed her to move so he wouldn't have to make up something.

Just as he was about to look at Wes, to gauge what was considered insubordination, she moved haltingly. He was fascinated and intrigued. His shirt was far too big on her, but even as it draped over her body, the crew neck kept her breasts from sight. Even so, their sway as she moved was evident. The hemline eased up over her ass, leaving her bare. Glints of glitter—most likely from her bed—twinkled. She wasn't graceful. There was no hint of seduction in her movements. Her unkempt hair was a tangled mess down her back and shoulders, but he was mesmerized.

He'd seen Narlina crawl, though not like this, never like this. He'd never ordered her to crawl, but she'd moved around on all fours on the floor when she'd played with Ruff. It had never been sexual, alluring. This shouldn't be either. A captive woman forced to crawl across the room on command, every movement stilted and rich with devastation. Her reluctance was palpable. But she was doing it, following his order.

His cock was stiffening.

Revenge. He was hard at the thought. At the suggestion of how much this moment would hurt Narlina. The very existence of his prize was a taunt, and that's what turned him on: the thought of her pain overshadowing his.

Rogan released his breath when she came to a halt in front of Wes.

Wes smiled down at her and tucked a knuckle under her chin, forcing her head back. When he'd positioned her where he wanted her, she kept her focus set on Wes's chest; she wouldn't meet his gaze. Her nostrils flared, and her back moved up and down violently; she was breathing hard. Though the color on her cheeks wasn't from exertion.

Was she mad? Embarrassed?

It didn't matter.

Wes leaned back in the chair, resting his hand on the button on his jeans, and sent a look of quiet permission to him.

Rogan assessed each of them. She hadn't moved, but her gaze had dropped to Wes's hand. He couldn't be sure, but he thought she'd stopped breathing; tension shot through the air, and it wasn't Wes or him.

Slowly, Rogan nodded.

Wes grinned, returning his attention to her, and unfastened his jeans. "You remember how I like it."

Wes pulled his dick out and stroked it slowly once, twisting his hand up and squeezing the tip. He held himself there for a moment before sliding back down and gripping the base. Rogan wanted to reach for his own cock but resisted the urge. Wes fisted her tangled hair and yanked her forward; she opened her mouth, understanding her assignment. Rogan's pulse leaped as Wes's cock disappeared. When Wes groaned, Rogan stopped himself from mimicking the sound.

"Fuck, Doll. I've been waiting for this."

His friend stared down at her taking his dick, his look of rapture and delight one Rogan hadn't seen on his friend before. And he'd seen Wes get plenty of blow jobs; he'd seen his friend fuck and get fucked. He'd jerked him off himself, sucked the dick his prize was now working. Yet he'd never seen that look on Wes's face, like he was slipping his dick into nirvana instead of a random slave's mouth.

"Oh, fuck. Oh, Jesus."

He orchestrated her pace; tears were rolling down her cheeks, and with every few strokes, she gagged. When she swallowed, it sent Wes into panting fits, since it coincided with his dick hitting the back of her throat—she was swallowing his cock.

It was violent; she braced herself on the floor as his hand slammed her mouth down on him. Over and over.

"Take it. Take it all."

Snot, slobber, tears, the sound of her choking... It was beautiful, the way he fucked her mouth, as messy as it was. But Wes liked to make a mess.

He grunted, his hand fisting as he tensed and released into her. He came and came; she made a sound of protest, struggling against the hand holding her in place as her throat was filled, cum dribbling out of her mouth.

Finally, Wes collapsed against the chair and shoved her head away. He dropped his own back, gasping for air. She remained on all fours, eyes wide and shell-shocked. She trembled, drool and cum leaking out of her mouth. The interaction had been savage, and possibly the sexiest thing Rogan had ever seen. His cock was aching.

Rolling his head on the chair back, Wes looked over at him, his blue eyes shining. "You're next."

Rogan shook his head. He'd already stopped himself more than once from using her; he wanted to hold on to his rage, his anger, and his hurt. Giving in to her mouth, her ass, or her cunt, would show weakness.

Wes was out of the chair like a shot, shoving his dick back in his pants. He was a blur of energy and motion, grasping her arm as she cowered. She let out a sharp squeal from fright or pain—maybe both. Rogan's friend approached him, the sex sheen gone from his eyes, and slid her across the floor to land at his feet.

Sitting back in his chair, arms crossed, Rogan dragged his steely gaze from Wes to his pet and back.

"Take out your cock."

Rogan scoffed.

"This is yours. Take her. Mark her. *Own her.*"

"I don't need—"

"Her, or me."

Rogan forced a smile. He enjoyed it when Wes tried to dominate him. "I don't need to own you; I already do." He also liked to push Wes to action; it got him even harder.

Wes didn't disappoint. He dropped her arm, and Rogan had barely registered her curling in on herself when Wes tackled him. They almost went over, the chair tilting on two legs as Wes yanked him out of it.

Rogan struggled, knocking into the table. The beer bottles rocked, threatening to topple over and spill onto the surface. But his concentration was on Wes, on battling him, and on the lust his friend's roughness sent coursing through him. They were matched when it came to strength, but Rogan was at the disadvantage, having started from a seated position.

Eventually, Wes had him where he wanted him: on his back, on the table, sweatpants wrangled down around his thighs. His cock was pulsing with need, bobbing from their efforts. Wes gripped the base, causing Rogan to jerk and let out a low groan.

Leaning over him, Wes gave his dick two quick pulls. "Let me give her to you."

Rogan wrapped his hand around Wes's, shaking his head. "I'll take you."

"If you mark her, Narlina sees."

God, his heart. It cracked at the sound of her name. She'd fucking annihilated his heart. And he wanted to do the same to her. Wes's hot hand on his cock, sure and quick, was sending him close to release, his balls drawing up; it was fucking with his brain. But Wes was right: it would destroy her as he'd been destroyed.

Rogan relented. One nod.

"Fuck yeah!" Wes's hand disappeared as he backed away.

Rogan splayed his hands on the surface of the table, adjusting his stability.

"Stay there," Wes ordered. He bent, then drew her up with him. She stumbled, her eyes wide. She knew exactly what was about to happen.

Wes unceremoniously wiped her face, still wet with tears, snot, saliva, and cum. He transferred the moisture, sliding his hand between her thighs. She startled, taking a step backward. He let go of her only long enough to deliver a slap to her buttocks.

The sound reverberated through the room, mingling with her sniffles and his rough, anticipatory breaths. A heartbeat later, it was followed by a second berating spanking. The echo of her flesh being slapped made him harder.

Wes lifted her, guiding her over Rogan. She automatically bent her knees, understanding. Rogan didn't think for a minute she was willing, not by the fear in her eyes or the downturned line of her mouth, but her consent wasn't required. All he needed from her was her pussy.

He braced himself on his elbows, watching. Wes grasped Rogan's cock, lining him up, orchestrating. He had one arm around her waist, holding her steady over his dick.

Above him, her eyes were squeezed tightly closed, as though staring into the void wouldn't be enough to take her away from this moment. Cum and snot were smeared and drying on her face; her hair was stringy and hanging limply. She was still strangely beautiful, about to be speared.

He didn't owe her grace or leniency, this pitiful replacement for a life stolen from him. His cock was eager and ready, even more so at the heat of her above him. He could imagine the warm sheath of her. Surely a few bounces would give him a moment's reprieve from the hellscape he was relegated to with her. So it was fitting she bear this with him, right?

"No!" Rogan slapped his hands on the table and slid back, slid out from under her. He sat up on its surface and shivered as Wes subsequently released him.

He wasn't sure who looked more startled: Wes or her. Wes's brows were high with shock, though his jaw was rigid. He was pissed off. Before she dropped her gaze, but after her eyes had flown open at his sudden movement, disbelief and relief had washed over her. The relief was for the reprieve. He understood that. But the disbelief? Maybe because she knew this was only one of many misses. He could change his mind at any time.

"Ro!" Wes berated.

"She doesn't get to turn me into a rapist."

Wes's face screwed up. "She doesn't turn you into anything; she's *yours*."

Rogan tucked his legs and spun, vacating the table, and yanked up his sweatpants. "I meant Narlina." Taking several steps away from them, keeping his back turned, he ran his shaking hands through his hair. "She's made me her servant *and* an owner of flesh. But she won't turn me into a person like our guests in the fancy bungalows."

"She wants it."

With a scoff, Rogan stumbled over to the sink. The look on her face was the exact opposite of the expression someone who *wanted it* would make.

Towel in hand, he held it under the tap. After all the trouble he'd gone to in order to get her clean, her face was filthy. As he wrung out the cloth, he glanced over his shoulder.

Wes was nuzzling her neck, playful and mischievous. She was malleable in his arms, of course she was, but her attention had been on Rogan, as evidenced by the way her eyes dropped quickly when he looked.

Between playful nips along her neck and shoulder, Wes peered up at him. "Pillow talk is enlightening. Fantasies of kidnap, rape, and being forced into submission." Grinning, focus still on Rogan, he tugged on her earlobe with his teeth.

Rogan folded the rag, studying her blank expression. Intimate moments whispered to a person she thought was a lover had been taken and turned against her. He didn't want to know about Wes's betrayal of her beyond the obvious. It gave her and him a commonality.

He threw the rag at them. "Clean her up."

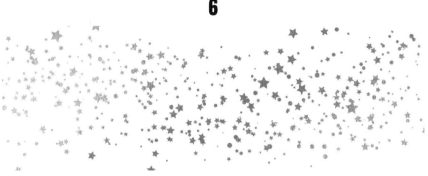

DENIAL

The Prize

There had been an infamous island in the news; the stories had been sensational. Media fodder. Until it was squelched. With all the terrible things going on in the world, it was easy to distract the populace from the detestable acts that occurred there. There had been a cable documentary or two, but largely it had been hushed. Celebrity divorces were pushed to the fore.

She'd been no different from the general public, shocked at first, unable to wrap her head around the concept of it, telling herself she was too worldly and independent to fall prey to the schemes of nefarious men. By nature, she was suspicious and hypervigilant. But she had become distracted by her own reality: bills and classes—all immediate and relevant in her life. The idea of a sex trade or sex trafficking was preposterous, far-fetched. She was too wary to be caught up in it herself.

Yet here she was, kneeling on a table and wrapped in the arms of the man responsible for her abduction. He was right: this was what she'd wanted.

What was the saying? Be careful what you wish for?

Though this wasn't exactly what she'd wished for. She thought she'd been sharing her innermost secrets with a man who cared about her, who could provide for her safety.

The heat between her legs was meaningless, as was the jolt of arousal that had overtaken her as he'd positioned her over Rogan, her owner. The responses were involuntary, she rationalized, caused by adrenaline and conditioning. Wes hadn't needed to use their bodily fluids to lubricate her; it occurred naturally. Attributed to some deep-seated desire, as Wes had revealed, further betraying her. Or maybe her body was trying to protect her by giving her the ability to take some part of this for herself so it wouldn't hurt so badly.

It hurt. And she was scared. Wes had shredded her heart, but that ache was insignificant in the face of all she'd endured since. He'd evaporated more quickly than he should have from her consciousness—the sweet, caring man who'd plowed through her defenses—but she'd been facing far bigger obstacles.

She hadn't expected to see him again. No, she assumed she'd be sold off to some foreign land, if she wasn't in a foreign land already. Everyone she had encountered spoke English, but that didn't mean anything. Seeing him today resurrected the hurt, the anger. In a fucked-up corner of her brain, there had been a shred of hope that he was here to right the wrongs.

But he'd degraded her. Used her. Was offering her to his friend, like an eager boy wanting to share a favorite toy. And now he was trying to be playful with her. He had always been playful after sex. Now, though, how did he not notice that it wasn't appreciated? Maybe he did; maybe he didn't care.

But his comment was accurate. She had wanted to experiment, to test the boundaries of her newfound appreciation for sex. She'd trusted him then, and she had been curious.

Rogan was handsome, with his dark looks and a few days' scruff. She shouldn't be thinking this way, but there were worse men or women who could own her.

She'd heard about Stockholm syndrome. Even learned a bit in a college course. She didn't identify with these men, however. There was no sympathy for them.

Wes reached for the moist towel Rogan had tossed. Her face was itchy with tears and cum. Yes, she'd cried; his cock had been choking her. The gagging brought tears to her eyes, and her fight for air had forced the snot out.

Unceremoniously, Wes scrubbed at her face.

With a sudden movement, she was pulled from the table. She stumbled as she tried to stand, causing Wes to pull her in close. It felt like his gesture was one of instinct, to keep her from falling and harming herself, but if so, that was in contrast to her very presence here.

"Put her back."

The directive from Rogan was accompanied by a jerk of his chin to indicate her bed in the corner. Relief flowed through her; it was another reprieve.

Wes turned her in his arms and smiled at her. Her heart stumbled. The stupid organ had yet to comprehend that he was no longer a love interest. That his pretty eyes and grin were dipped in duplicity and depravity.

"Okay, Doll, back to your corner." Then he kissed her. A real one. It was surreal. She went rigid in his arms, not that he seemed to notice.

Turning her again, this time so she faced her bed, he delivered another smack to her ass. It smarted only slightly less due to the t-shirt. "Go on."

She wouldn't dally or wait for another command to crawl. Her mind had rebelled against that disturbing order. She quickly repressed the images speeding through her head, that it was a seductive act in movies and novels.

She wouldn't consider that they found her alluring as she'd fought every natural sway of her body as she'd moved.

Released, she scurried for her bed with such speed she was surprised the men hadn't laughed. Once she'd dropped to the soft surface, she wedged herself into the corner, drawing her knees up and watching them watch her.

"She isn't sleeping there, is she?"

Rogan shrugged. "Why not?"

Wes raised a brow. "You're going to give her free rein of your place while you sleep?"

She hadn't thought of it, but now it was on all of their minds. She had access to the kitchen where, presumably, she could find a weapon. And the front door was just across the room.

Would she run away?

To where? She didn't know where she was, so it was impossible to know where she could run to. But both men were looking at her like she was capable of actions she'd never before contemplated. How desperate was she? Quite. But she also wasn't stupid.

Rogan glowered at her, as though she'd announced her intent to kill him in his sleep.

Wes shook his head. "I brought you a few things." He wandered over to the sofa, where a duffel bag lay. "You're unprepared."

"I wasn't supposed to *be* here," the other man groused. "I also didn't get an owner's manual."

Wes withdrew an item she couldn't quite make out and threw her a wink. Then he held up what turned out to be a pair of leather wrist cuffs. "Practical for more reasons than one. You'll want her hands incapacitated. Perhaps tie her to the bed."

Next, he produced a pair of yoga pants.

Rogan frowned, his brows lowered in suspicion. "You have clothes for her?"

"Yeah. I was ready. After you were gone, she was supposed to keep *me* company. Do you think I'd want any asshole thinking they had a right to her?" Wes shook the pants. "These are to keep men from sticking their dicks in her when she's outside your apartment."

"No one touches what's mine," Rogan said, his chin raised and his jaw rigid. In another situation, his response could be considered one of protectiveness, but this was pure selfish possession.

"If you flash her pussy at them, it's an invitation. I know you're hung up on Narlina right now, but my doll here is fucking gorgeous," Wes countered. "Dress her."

She was aware of Rogan's deepening curiosity. Meanwhile, she hardened herself against Wes's declaration, knowing it didn't mean anything. At least she didn't want his words to affect her in a way that made her heart skip.

"Feed her, give her water, clean her," Wes prattled off.

"I know how to fucking take care of a—" He startled, his eyes going wide.

Her heart rate picked up as she assessed him. What had he been about to call her? Woman? Person? Slave?

"Ro. Man. Don't take your shit out on her."

Rogan's eyes narrowed. "Ten minutes ago, you were trying to drop her on my cock."

Wes massaged the back of his neck. "I didn't say not to fuck her."

• • • • • • • • •

He cuffed her to the bed, but not in the way she'd expected. After dragging her bed into his bedroom, he plopped it on the floor, directed her onto it with a pointed finger, and secured her wrists around the foot of his bed.

It wouldn't be the most comfortable position, but she'd sleep better than she had since being taken. She had a soft bed, even if it was small. She was clean and more properly fed after Wes had made her a sandwich (his Jekyll/Hyde kindnesses were disconcerting), and she had used the bathroom under her owner's curious and watchful eye. He'd dropped a blanket carelessly over her, so she was warm, too.

He ignored her after that, reminding her of her insignificance, of her status as a prop. Eventually, she'd be a toy. She had no illusions about that. She might have escaped tonight, the games they would play with her, but her reprieve would be short-lived.

He stripped, disappeared down the hall. He took a piss, then turned on the water. Hygiene, she imagined: hands washed and teeth brushed. The same routine he'd made her go through after producing a toothbrush for her. She didn't know whether it was new or even if it had belonged to the dog whose bed she'd been relegated to. It hadn't tasted bad, at least.

Wes finally left them. She said "them" only because he had asked for a pile-up in the bed.

Rogan had shaken his head. "I need my head tonight."

"You *need* head tonight," Wes fired back.

The men had stared at one another, taut tension, a pull, tugging at them. Wes took one step toward his friend before Rogan had stopped him with another shake of his head. "Another time."

So Wes had headed for the door, winking at her on his way. "Be good to him."

As though he was unaware of her circumstances—as though he wasn't the one who had dragged her into this distorted reality. Though dragged was the wrong word. She'd allowed herself to be led without rebellion.

After Rogan's bathroom routine, she was plunged into darkness and silence. He padded across the room; seconds later, the bed squeaked and shifted. But the movement wasn't enough to be that of a man lying down. Sitting on the side, perhaps?

Through the pounding of her heart, which was likely audible in the dark sterility, she heard his heavy sigh. She imagined he was sitting, his head in his hands. But she wouldn't move; she wouldn't remind him of her presence any more than she was certain he was already aware.

When the room filled with what sounded like the broken breaths of silent tears, she eased a fraction. Maybe her existence had been forgotten. Thankful probably wasn't the right word, but it was the closest label she could come up with. Emotions, for her, had never been easily identifiable. Not before Wes. And now? Now, she wasn't sure what she felt. Relief, of course, to be insignificant rather than be used as an outlet for his pain.

Scared. Fear overshadowed every thought and every action. Relief in this moment was just that—for this moment alone. Her experiences had been and would continue to be measured in tiny moments in which she could find respite.

Physical pain and discomfort would be companions, but this foam bed was better than sitting up naked in a cold cage. She was bewildered, of course. That hadn't changed.

But his tears, sorrow over the loss of another person—Narlina; a girl-friend?—imbued him with a level of humanity she hadn't entertained he'd had. Yes, he'd refused to fuck her, but she'd only been in his possession for less than a day. There was time, and she wasn't stupid enough to think it wouldn't happen. It was her entire purpose. Her body was his reward.

For what, she didn't know, and it didn't matter. Answers weren't hers to demand.

He hadn't stopped Wes, either; wouldn't stop Wes.

A break, a crack, a part of her brain that terrified her more than the situation she'd found herself in, mocked her. Because she hadn't wanted him to stop Wes. In a sense, Wes was a known entity, and there was a fucked-up comfort in that.

Embrace the devil you know; that sort of thing.

As much as she despised him for doing this to her, to a point, she knew what to expect from him. Or maybe she was fooling herself. Because what he'd done to her was not anything she could have imagined the charming man she'd quickly fallen for was capable of.

Yet here she was, cuffed to a bedpost, grateful for the momentary reprieve. Tonight, at least, there would be no punishments. No torturous contraptions that forced her body or mouth into compliance. The cuffs weren't hurting her. She'd gladly take this over the nightmares of the past weeks.

So she lay in the darkness, surrounded by the sounds of his heavy breathing, his lament for the life he'd lost when he'd won her. She'd cost him. He *would* take it out on her. The question was when.

7

COLLAR

Rogan

He wanted to wring the tears from his slave so he could imagine Narlina's tears falling along with them. Mainly, he wanted someone else to hurt as much as he did; she could provide the outlet. Fuck Wes and his warning. He'd given her to Rogan, and now Rogan could use her how he saw fit.

These were the thoughts that surged to the forefront of his mind as he watched his prize sleeping, curled into a ball at the base of his bed, as though she were content to be treated like the dog on whose bed she slept. Her oblivion annoyed him. He'd cried all night, his heart breaking so badly he wasn't certain he'd wake up a full man.

In fact, he wasn't certain he was completely intact. He rubbed his chest, knowing it wasn't a physical pain, but it felt physical.

He shoved at the thick foam mattress with his foot. "Get up."

She startled and gasped, her body jolting. The chain linking the cuffs clinked against the frame as she attempted to sit up. Blinking wearily, half of her snarled hair in her face, she looked up at him. The dazed look she gave him was alluring. There was a red pressure mark on her cheek emphasized by gold glitter. That shit was going to be a bitch to get rid of.

Wes was right, though: she was gorgeous.

But she wasn't Narlina. Or freedom.

He tore his gaze from her face, not bothering to reprimand her for looking at him, and glared at the cuffs. Fuck. Where'd he leave the key?

With a curse, he left the room to search for it. He didn't have to look long. It was in the bag Wes had brought for her. Rogan would think about it later, how prepared Wes had been. How much thought his friend had put into having her with him. Taking her for himself was a risk. There was no guarantee he'd get to keep her. Wes was popular, he procured quality merchandise, but that didn't mean he was given many favors.

Unlike himself.

It'd been a smart, strategic move, even if it hadn't been planned, for Wes to give her to Rogan.

Rogan paused in his return to the bedroom. It *hadn't* been planned, had it? Wes had been as surprised as he was at the sudden turn of events. Right? Shaking his head, he forced the paranoia aside; Wes wouldn't sabotage him like that, especially at a cost to himself. Narlina's betrayal was fucking with his mind. After what she'd done, he would see enemies everywhere. Except, ironically, in the woman now kneeling on her bed.

Wasn't that a kick in the balls? His slave was the only one who hadn't conspired against him. It didn't mean he owed her anything. Again, she was symbolic of what he was: trapped here as much as she.

When he crouched and grabbed her wrist, she surveyed him quickly, only to seek out another part of the room an instant later, her cheeks coloring. Not that he cared about her embarrassment, but it was odd, wasn't it? Should a sex slave blush?

The cuffs dropped to the floor. Even though they were leather-padded sex cuffs instead of metal, she still rubbed at her wrists as though circulation had been cut off; it hadn't been. Grasping her arm, startling another intake of air from her, he dragged her to her feet.

In the bathroom, he motioned to the toilet. She hesitated, head down, the red in her cheeks heightening. It wasn't a turn-on, watching her pee, not like one would imagine. Her humiliation was what he ate up, her lack of control, the sense of power it gave him.

Yesterday morning, the thought would have made him ill. Now, he craved her torment as a mirror of his own; would use her suffering to salve himself. He wouldn't reflect on how easy it was to succumb to the darkness, like it had been lying beneath the surface, ready for an excuse to welcome him home.

He hadn't wanted to be swallowed by the horrors around him; Narlina had been his light, his faith, his guiding star. But she'd anchored him in hell; knowingly, with forethought.

So be it. He was now Narlina's creation, and her unintentional gift would answer for her sins.

• • • • • • • • •

Rogan snarled as he shoved his newly fixed pet toward her bed in the corner. A trip to the clinic should have been simple. Instead, she had been grabbed and fondled. The place had been filled with an air of curiosity and the need to explore her, experience her, as though they had the right to touch her.

Her scared, startled brown eyes had sought him out every time—three times in all—begging for his intervention. He had intervened, but not for her sake. No one was allowed to touch what belonged to him without his permission. Why it bothered him, their hands on her came down to one thing, or so he told himself, she was his pet. And he wasn't in the mood to share her or talk about her. It didn't matter that slaves were regularly shared. He hadn't invited them to do so. Therefore they shouldn't have assumed.

Instead of insisting she walk behind him, he'd been forced to lead her by the hand; the link signaled that she wasn't to be bothered. No one would dare pull her from his grasp. The only thing that kept him powering from one building to the next, her hand clutching his, was the thought that somewhere, somehow, Narlina might be watching.

He wanted her to see a connection that didn't exist, care that wasn't there.

He wanted her hurt.

His mood hadn't improved once they'd arrived at the clinic. He was given the options for her birth control. Like, what the fuck? She'd lain on the table looking shell-shocked, eyes fixed on the ceiling, as he was given his choices.

This was a task he should have left to Wes. Instead, *just as with every other fucking thing in the past day*, he was grappling with shit beyond his interest or ability. He'd gone with an IUD; it was fastest, didn't require pills or surgery.

Afterward, they'd tattooed a decorative *R* on her wrist, then the Roman numeral I, because she was his first. The barcode was worthless beyond a visual reminder that she was property. A product.

Now back at his apartment, he stalked over to a kitchen drawer as she sank to her knees on her bed, which he'd made her drag back to the front room that morning. He rifled through the drawer, pulling out discarded collars, holding them up and measuring them for length. When he glanced over at her, she was eyeing him warily, but she quickly dropped her gaze.

The one he held was a soft brown leather. It almost matched her eyes. Ruff hadn't worn it; it'd been a gift. When people didn't know what to give a person, they bought something for that person's pet.

As he approached her, she stiffened. The reaction didn't slow him.

"Chin up," he instructed as he came to a stop in front of her.

She obeyed, her eyes locking on the collar. Her deep breaths indicated she understood what he intended to do with it. Without fanfare, he slid it around her neck. Her neck was long, pretty; it was smaller than Ruff's, so the leather settled easily. He fastened the clasp and stepped back to consider it on her.

His cock jumped. Fucking hell, her kneeling pose, the adornment... *his*. "Every pet needs a collar."

8

NORMALIZING

The Prize

She was aware enough of the world to know that if she'd been in a normal relationship, where it was negotiated and consented to, being collared would be an honor. This collaring was not that. This wasn't about honor or care. It was about possession.

His *pet*.

Except pets were usually liked by their owners. He didn't like her, even if he had angrily and aggressively shoved away people who had stroked her, felt her up. As strangers' hands had found their way to places they shouldn't go—she was still struggling with her shift in circumstance even after weeks in training—she had been thankful for Wes's foresight and the pants he'd provided. It was a thoughtfulness on his part, an attempt to protect. It was fucked up that he would preserve any part of her humanity or dignity—her body—after the situation he'd put her in. Her presence here alone showed his disregard for her.

It didn't matter what she'd told him about wanting this: wanting no control over her decisions, to be a pawn, to be used. She had imagined having the autonomy to give herself over to someone. This had been taken from her.

After Rogan collared her, though, he seemed content to ignore her. She didn't want his attention, but his utter contempt bothered her. That feeling was irritating. It was for the best, his dismissal of her, because her wrist throbbed, and the insertion was causing her to cramp. It was better to remain on her small bed and suffer in silence.

The woman at the clinic had given her what she assumed to be an aspirin. It had been a kindness, even if it didn't remove the pain's full effect. If this was the dulled version, she didn't think she would have been able to stay silent had this small mercy not been granted. As it was, she panted through the cramping.

Not unlike a dog. The irony wasn't lost on her.

Before she'd had a chance to divine the woman's motivation, the doctor shifted, and the cuff of her white coat rode up. She was marked with a tattoo similar to the one that had just been inked into her own skin, only the other looked like an *L*.

Rogan hadn't provided her with instructions after he walked away. She was determined to think of him as Rogan although he hadn't given her permission to refer to him as anything. She didn't want to think of him as her owner. If she did, it would reinforce the ownership. Of course, she wasn't allowed to speak, so it would be a moot point. But she liked rules and needed permission before she could comfortably think about him as Rogan. In this, she decided she would make an executive decision.

She didn't know the guidelines, her boundaries, the *rules* of being owned. Would her daily routine consist of only sitting on a dog bed? What would they do to her if she lost her mind, went mad? Kill her? Give her to someone else who didn't care if they fucked a woman out of her mind?

A couple of the people she had been caged with had broken down; lost their minds. *People* because not only women had been taken, although they were predominant. She'd seen individuals of all races, genders, identities, and ages—to a certain point, of course. But as a twenty-three-year-old white woman, she was an anomaly. She didn't resist. She didn't rebel or fight back like some had. It was natural to some, she supposed, but not to her. Comparatively, she was easy; she knew how to endure horror, to acquiesce to the unthinkable. This wasn't her first introduction to the cruelties of others.

In a sense, her childhood had trained her for this moment. Wes had seen it in her, recognized it. Used it. He'd needed a silent survivor, someone whose mind was strong enough to endure. And then he'd found her in a coffee shop.

9

VALUE

Rogan

He heard her whimpers. She buried her face in her bed, trying to disguise them, but he heard them, nevertheless. A part of him felt compelled to comfort her, as he would any other individual who was hurting. Like he would have held and cared for Narlina.

But he steeled himself against it, the compassion. If she hadn't been given to him, he wouldn't have been forced into the decision of causing her pain. It was a narcissistic view, and he knew it. He also couldn't help how much he blamed her for her existence. As if Narlina would have made another decision if his pet hadn't been a factor.

He shoved aside the knowledge that Narlina had been as surprised as he when the prize had tumbled to his feet. Along with the surprise was a flash of pain in her eyes. Yet she still hadn't reached out to him. Twenty hours of silence from the woman who'd claimed to love him, had wanted to run away with him, had sworn she was willing to risk all for the opportunity.

What clue had he missed?

His eyes had been fixed on the chute that would deliver salvation. His prize, his due: money. It would have been enough to buy his way out of here, off this island; both he and Narlina. She'd stood on the platform, taunting the crowd as she pretended to appear conflicted over which prize he'd earned.

All along, she knew. At least, he'd thought she knew. From the moment they'd understood what a depraved hellhole this place was, they'd dreamed about getting away. They'd been ignorant to the truth until he'd been sent to the mainland for technical training. During his time there, their alternative life had been brought into focus, and since then, he'd wanted nothing to do with it.

Narlina wanted to be free of her husband. It hadn't been easy. Not only was she married to the sick bastard who ran this place, but the island was under surveillance, and every resident had a GPS tracker implanted. Most weren't aware of this truth, but there wasn't a single person who'd been brought or born here who wasn't tagged. Others were part of a larger inventory with RFID devices embedded and tattooed. Only the guests were anonymous and unscathed. Identified, sure, and photographed for insurance purposes, but not marked.

It was to have ended for them, the sneaking, the fear of discovery. They would leave to live a normal life among the billions of other people walking the earth, no longer shackled to the distorted reality they'd been born into. They would go to Australia. It was surely far enough away, on the other side of the world. New names, new life.

Narlina had whirled on the platform, her sparkling blue dress catching his eye. He'd smiled. There was no reason to suppress it; it was a celebration, and he could be happy. The crowd expected him to smile. But he was smiling because he hadn't believed the moment when he could get away with her would ever come.

The plan had been foolproof. With Wes's assistance and his own knowledge regarding the technology, the trackers would have been removed. They would have disappeared into the masses on the mainland.

Free.

So he'd stood in the middle of the arena, bare-chested, in a pair of work boots and jeans. His fellow islanders crowded around, their anticipation and excitement palpable. Everyone enjoyed the gifting, the gifts. It was part of what kept them from rebelling, he suspected, the treats meant to entice and ground. There was so much more, of course.

The prize for him was to have been Narlina, because for him, *she* was perfect.

The signal was given by her husband, the man sitting on a dais behind Rogan. Rogan hadn't bothered to turn to look at him. Instead, he'd taken a deep breath, attempting to calm his pounding heart before it beat out of his chest.

Per tradition, his shirt had been removed to reveal the barcode tattooed on his right shoulder. Although the residents all knew him, and the barcode was obsolete, he had to be scanned before the gifting ceremony could begin. This was to maintain the lie that the barcode meant something. The scan was followed by the announcement of his name: Rogan. No last name. It was intentional, not providing the islanders with more than one name. It acted as another hurdle, another need for explanations: no identifying information, no birth certificates, no last names. No existence.

Of course, there were exceptions. Every ruler needed an educated population, no matter how small, to support the mechanism. Rogan was in communications. Wes worked for procurement, in all forms and in the broadest of interpretation.

A thrill had shot through him at the thought of gifting Narlina with a last name.

She'd stopped twirling, and her giggles subsided as she sobered, remembering her task.

The cheers doubled. Claps, stomping feet, and congratulatory shouts filled the air. The prize always varied. Rogan had seen everything from cash in various currencies to gold bars, which he would accept as happily. He'd seen bulk food, clothes, pets, entertainment systems, and slaves of all sexes, colors, and ages. The prize always matched the recipient's desire. Wants and needs could be simple or twisted. Regardless, the appropriate reward would find itself tumbling down the chute.

Narlina had taken her place between the two exaggerated levers and placed one hand on each knob. Her smile returned when the noise hit a fever pitch. In that moment, he'd felt and appreciated the love and support from his community, knew he was a favorite. At thirty, he had earned the respect and trust of almost every person here. Even the bastard behind him.

He would still leave them. With her.

Narlina had surveyed him. His heart had jumped. He'd hoped she could see his love—glimpses of their future—in his eyes.

Following the script, she'd teased the crowd by easing forward one lever, then pulling it back. Her hand tightened on one stick, and she diverted her focus to him again. His breath held. That was it, the lever that would deliver them.

But she'd given him that apologetic hint of a frown and pulled the other one.

Coming back to the present, he sought out his gift. She remained curled up in the corner, tensing occasionally against pain, those little whimpers escaping her. He needed to hate her. He needed her cries to echo the sounds of his own soul grieving his loss.

That would be her value: his outlet, a substitute for his loss.

10

REPRESSION

The Prize

Allowing her mind to venture anywhere but her reality, dividing her attention in such a way, was dangerous. She needed to have her wits about her at all times. But what else did she have to do once she'd been ordered to the corner, with no voice? She was forgotten until she wasn't. Vigilance against losing her mind was the higher priority, especially when no immediate threat was detectable, present situation notwithstanding.

The walk to the clinic (in retrospect, she was thankful he hadn't made her crawl), beyond the grabbing and groping that her owner had angrily defended her from, had been informative. No one appeared concerned by her presence, by her ability to take in her surroundings. As if they weren't worried about her escaping. As if there were no possibility. Between the sterile-looking buildings along their path, she'd glimpsed a vast body of water in the distance. It was a sunny day, and the heat was relentless. Though she kept her focus averted, too afraid to look at anyone's face, she noted that most people wore lighter clothing.

The tropics, maybe? Various palm trees supported her suspicion. But how far south? Where else did palm trees grow? The west coast? She was a far cry from where she'd originated, with chilly days and chillier evenings this time of year. At least, she didn't think she'd lost that much time. Did knowing this information help her situation? Spur ideas for ways to escape? No. It was useless. She had a tracker at the base of her hairline; that had been done on the boat. They'd tattooed evidence of his ownership on her wrist after she'd endured the placement of the IUD. And she had nowhere to run.

Before, her life hadn't been an exciting one, but she'd been content. Struggling, but making it. Defying the odds.

That's what taunted her; she'd survived so much, only for the horrors to leave an invisible mark on her for someone else to take up. Her independence, her solitude, her silent life: it was a beacon. Or maybe it was the after-sex conversations with a beautiful man who'd made her feel safe and cherished and loved.

She'd fallen so quickly and deeply into him, a testament to the need within her for connection, to be valued so she could validate herself through him. If he loved her, she was lovable; that love would erase all the years of being told she was worthless, that her existence was a burden.

No one is your friend. No one likes you. They're just using you. You'd be stupid to let them. The sentiment had been sneered repeatedly. She didn't want to believe it; she wanted friends, but she'd never known how to connect. Still, she tried. But her gauge was off, and that had allowed Wes to take advantage of her vulnerability years later.

A devastating example? Ann. A colleague before they became friends. Because Ann had said they were friends, so it must have been true. Her desperate need for approval overrode the warning signs that Ann was manipulating her for her own gain. After torturous months of trying to reconcile empty words to actions, she was forced to acknowledge the truth: she was being used. She was familiar with love bombing, should have recognized the tactic, but a narcissist knows how to affect the emotionally vulnerable.

It had been a crippling blow to admit her stupidity, that those childhood lessons had forewarned this. She'd allowed Ann to use her as her launching pad, to be the one to propel the woman forward, providing the boost until her friend moved on to *better*, and she was no longer useful. The callous disposal of her made her feel like shit on Ann's shoe to be flicked off.

Not good enough, not good enough, never good enough.

Still, she'd vied for approval, to please, to rebuild a connection that, for Ann, had never existed. She'd eventually raged and pleaded, only to have her feelings cruelly disregarded. To be blamed, even, for having the audacity to feel slighted. It was a wasted effort. Ann's sights were on other, more golden prizes (yes, she recognized the irony). Her friend left her. Once the rocket fuel, she'd been left to dissipate into the ether.

Although aware of the tactics of narcissists, the unnecessary additional cruelty of talking behind her back left her baffled. She was no one, with no power, so she hadn't been certain what satisfaction the woman had gained by doing it. Then again, life had taught her that narcissists hated having a mirror held up to them. She should have known better, but profound hurt had driven her. It also reinforced that people weren't good and that there was truth in those earlier, snarled words.

After, to counter her self-loathing for her stupidity, she'd scrambled to point to evidence of her intelligence: surviving on her own, paying her bills (barely), and getting into a master's program. She'd worked hard to be acknowledged for that intelligence—she'd been an honor student—but it wasn't enough. She craved recognition and acceptance, but no matter what she did, she never won anyone over. Not unless she did their bidding. Even then, their appreciation was fleeting.

So, of course, Wes had used her. Because the truth remained. No one wanted to be her friend; she was stupid. But she'd had a lifetime of experience being a tool.

Now, as she watched her owner pace the room, blasting text after text on his cell phone, she wasn't only a tool. She had become *his* burden.

He stopped and considered his phone's screen, then threw it onto the sofa with a growl. His nostrils flared, and he sucked in air like a drowning man who'd made it to the surface: desperate, wild.

If she were drowning, she'd suck in the water.

No, her mind rebelled. She was a survivor. She'd escape this reality. At least she'd tell herself that, even though, deep down, she knew the only escape was through death. Now, or later. It was the interim she should be concerned about, how she would be led to that death.

An image from a television show popped into her brain, one where the whores were shot through with a crossbow because it amused their king. Rogan was now her king; what amused him?

The individuals responsible for her life—this life—had been amused by torment and torture, without reason or cause. They hadn't needed a reason beyond the perceived cost of bringing her into the world. Her, and the others they brought into their home under the guise of fostering and caring.

One by one, the new lambs had been brought into her home to suffer tragically, only to be spit back out. More times than she wanted to recount, she'd been witness to unjustified beatings, the victim tied to a pole in the basement and beaten until bruised; they'd been set up for it. It had been a joke to the monster who'd raised her.

She'd maintained composure while atrocious sins had been conducted around her. Her smile was brilliant. Strangers would make remarks about how happy she was; it was no wonder she couldn't identify her emotions. Not when her soul was screaming for mercy, all while she was being told she was happy. It had been confusing, especially for a child. But her silence was compliance. She was as much a child as those lambs, equally dependent and without resources. Even so, she'd paid for her life—the one they'd given her—by being complicit. Her continued silence was interpreted as approval.

All she'd known then was that she had to survive. Count the years, months, and hours until she could escape. When she finally had, she'd been so proud of herself. Until one kind smile sent her back into a nightmare, as powerless as she'd been as a child.

Her entire existence had been based on the foundation of what she had cost or what another person could get out of her. So naturally, his comment to her the day he won her—*Do you know what you cost me?*—was a type of statement she was accustomed to. She understood that she deserved punishment because of it. No, she hadn't known what she cost him. She still didn't. But she'd learned early in life that every breath she took came at a price.

But *these* people didn't get to take credit for her obedience. They hadn't taught or beat or fucked anything out of her. She had been made for this moment. They might benefit from her upbringing, but they weren't the first monsters she'd encountered. No, they were just the ones she might not survive.

11

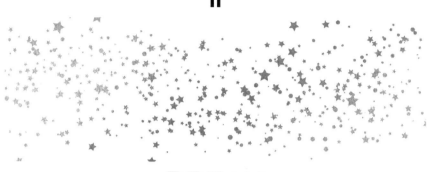

BREAK

Rogan

Narlina wasn't responding.

He'd finally texted her. His message was benign, because contacting her could be dangerous. In the text, he thanked her and Alan (though it galled him) for their generosity. He figured it would get a rise out of her, but his missive didn't elicit a response. He *wanted* to go to their bungalow and demand an audience. He wanted to force her hand. But it would only lead to destruction. More destruction, he amended, because he'd already been annihilated.

He needed answers, although her hiding from him spoke volumes. Maybe she was afraid of him, of his reaction. She should be. If she appeared right now, he'd strangle her for robbing him of what he'd—they'd—wanted and earned. And for ripping his heart out of his chest.

The worst of these sins, he didn't know. Was it being trapped here, or the loss of her love? He'd lived here his entire life; he probably could have been content remaining if he still had her in his life.

No, that wasn't true. He desired life on the mainland above all, with or without Narlina. Maybe it was a reaction to what had happened, but his focus was now firmly fixed on escaping. And an escape it would have to be. He couldn't stay on this island without wanting revenge. Hell, he wanted it now.

Without the money, he was stranded. And her position as the overseer's wife meant she would be in charge of any future offerings. *This* prize had been out of her control, and she would make damn certain it wasn't repeated.

He ran his hands through his hair and exhaled loudly. A slight movement in the corner caught his attention. His gift, his prize, his reward, his fucking future presented as flesh and blood.

Aware of his attention, she froze. She'd been scratching her thigh, judging from the red marks left by her fingernails, her hand still poised. She was pulling in long, steady breaths, but her pulse was racing. He could see the way it beat in the hollow of her neck. Her eyes were fixed on her knees, which were pulled up in front of her as she leaned back against the wall.

Other than his t-shirt, she was naked. Her round ass was visible, though her feet were tucked close enough together to hide her cunt. It didn't matter. He remembered well enough what her pussy looked like. And how his body had responded.

His cock stirred now, surely brought on by the rage inside him. It fueled a desire to fuck this toy with the image of Narlina's stricken face driving him on. He had every right to do whatever he wanted with her. Hell, Wes had already had his bit of fun and would be coming back for more.

As he stalked over to her, her body went rigid, but she didn't move.

She was smart. She knew how to make herself invisible, watched non-verbal cues. He crouched and grasped her chin, forcing her to face him. Her eyes, however, landed on his neck and stayed.

He reveled for a moment in her fear of him. The sensation sent adrenaline rushing through him. He could do anything he wanted to her without consequence; he felt powerful. Before him was a beautiful, terrified woman who had no choice but to absorb his fury. Until this moment, he wasn't aware he'd been missing it, this desire to overpower.

"Look at me," he growled. He wanted her eyes on him; he wanted to see her pupils dilate as he itemized her sins. Her attention immediately shifted, and then he was staring into a hypnotic brown abyss. The jolt that hit him took him off guard, but he forcibly shoved the sensation away, preferring to cling to anger. "Do you know what being here cost me? Do you know what was taken from me because of you? Do you think your pretty little pussy is worth my freedom? My happiness? Can your mouth suck me so good I forget where I *should* be?"

To her credit, her expression remained blank rather than pointing out the irony of his words.

Releasing her chin, he grasped her legs and turned her body toward him. Her lips parted to draw in breath at the sudden movement, but she didn't take her eyes from him, or make a sound. "This, this... this is all mine." He spat out the words, all the while grasping her breasts through the t-shirt. He dropped his hands to her thighs and shoved her legs apart.

"All mine, but I don't want you... *this*." He paused, his fingers at her entrance, his heart lurching. Because she was wet. He blinked, taken aback. Adrenaline might make her nipples hard, but it wouldn't make her wet, would it? Her eyes were still on him, a flush creeping up her cheeks.

Was she embarrassed that he'd discovered how much she enjoyed this? And which part turned her on? The words or the rough treatment? Both? Wes's statement, that she'd wished for a scenario like this in their shared past, rang in his mind.

He shoved his fingers inside her, breaching a physical and mental barrier. Her body tensed around him, and a low sound escaped her that made his cock stiffen. But he would deny himself. He was content to finger-fucking her slowly, astonished by her body's responses, oddly proud that he could elicit this from her. Proud, though the feeling was mixed with desperation and fury.

"I want to break you. I want you broken." He wanted it so he wouldn't be alone in being broken. He'd exercise cognitive dissonance, because he both hated her and wanted to have this commonality between them; he'd make her share it with him while he refused to acknowledge her pain, her torment. It was selfish, but Narlina had created a bitter, selfish, angry man.

The yielding expression on his prize told him she understood his words even as her pussy squeezed his thrusting fingers. Her nipples beaded beneath the white shirt, and goosebumps erupted on her skin. Her breath was fractured; her gaze clung to his; her hands gripped the mat beneath her. Her pelvis rocked, though only slightly, as if she wanted to lift and ride his hand. Maybe she did.

"You little whore; your cunt is craving this." They both knew it.

His words didn't dampen her responses. The room filled with her scent and the sound of his working her, getting her juices flowing as he drove his fingers into her faster.

Leaning in, he whispered against her ear. "My dirty little prize."

His words were answered with her panting and a soaking of his fingers. She tightened around him as she tried to stifle her cry, attempting to adhere to his rules. He continued to push into her, his thumb working her clit. That's all it took for her to fall apart. All the while, she struggled to maintain her silence, pressing her lips together and breathing through her nose. It wasn't completely working, but he noted her attempt.

It was sexy, witnessing her undoing while she wore the collar, a testament of his ownership. Her flush was glorious. Her pleading eyes made him feel powerful. Her tremors were delicious.

Fuck. How hard would his dick get if she were cuffed *and* collared and finding her release like this? Based on the stiffness now, he'd be fucking granite.

12

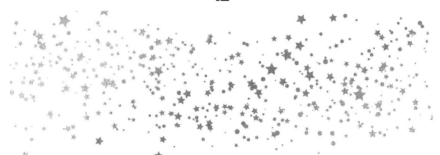

TRANSFERENCE
The Prize

Her cum coated his fingers. The orgasm had ripped through her like a well-rehearsed orchestra. Wes had provided her first orgasm to which she had consented, though he hadn't been the first to make her come. Her body had learned long ago how to accept the pleasure sex could provide, to take refuge in it amid the ugliness that created it.

The pleasure this man provided gave her that reprieve from her situation; it didn't shame her, the orgasm. Her sex drive had always been high. When stressed, she'd masturbate in an attempt to distract and soothe herself. Her pussy was conditioned to get wet when stressors were triggered, and this situation was the definition of triggering. Was her sexual response due to an introduction at an early age?

It had felt good, and the understanding that it was wrong hadn't been innate at first. The internal alarm had only begun to alert her after her perpetrators had told her it was wrong. They'd tried to assuage their guilt by confessing to her, a child; they justified their actions as they violated her, used her.

Would she have known, otherwise, that it was wrong? Would she have kept their secrets anyway, like they begged her to do, making her responsible for their sins?

It was confusing, to know for sure, because though she'd known it was an act she shouldn't be comfortable with—and many times, wasn't—she couldn't deny that she'd liked it sometimes. The attention, more than anything, was her reward: the praise she received, and her ability to please another person.

Most often, they'd blame her for their actions: she was pretty, tiny, good, quiet, tight. With every one, they reasoned that they couldn't help themselves. It was all her fault, for being a myriad of things that turned her partners on.

So this scenario with Rogan was not new. His hatred of her was unique. But her body responded the same now as it had in the past: eager to please. She wanted his praise, his acceptance. It was how she'd survived before; it was how she would survive this. Endure, at least, until there was nothing left to outlive.

The orgasm? The rush? She would take it every time. It was an escape, her own little prize, the momentary blacking out as her body convulsed with pleasure. She'd heard that an orgasm was like a small death. It would be the best way to die. The nightmare happened when she was resurrected from that death, when she remembered that she should be ashamed of her reaction.

Especially now, looking into the eyes of this man. Beneath the hurt and the anger, he was perplexed, like he wanted to explore her further, but he despised his curiosity.

She'd learned how to read people; she'd become a master at deciphering unspoken words. Her owner was easy to read, wearing his emotions openly. Of course, there was no reason to hide disdain.

He wasn't like Wes, who had slipped by her, barreling through her self-preservation. She'd so desperately wanted him to love her that she allowed herself to be blind. She'd neglected to look close enough, deep enough, because she didn't want to lose him.

Irony was everywhere.

Before her, Rogan brought his cum-covered fingers to his lips. He assessed her with a frown, as if trying to puzzle her out. Then he brought those fingers to his mouth and sucked her from them. Instantly, he startled, blinking rapidly, as though his actions had been more habit than intentional, and her taste in his mouth was new; unexpected.

But he didn't withdraw his hand. He slowly licked himself clean, becoming more... She thought the expression was one of intrigue, though maybe that was only what she wanted to see. She needed him to be interested. He was definitely studying her face. Could he see her desire to please? If he did, it would be her salvation, her next meal, his continued protection when she was groped and grabbed by strangers.

He moved suddenly, grasping her hips and yanking her to him. She tilted her head back to look up at him. Her heart thudded in dread and anticipation even as she got wetter. He was beautiful in his pain, even though that pain was turned on her.

"I don't care how good you taste, Prize," he spat the last word. "I'll always hate you." Scowling, he took her in again. "Even when I'm fucking you."

It wasn't the threat he'd intended. She interpreted his words to mean he wanted her. Hope bloomed. The fucked-up part of her brain was pleased that he liked the taste of her; she latched on to the positive, the praise. He liked one small aspect of who she was, albeit unwillingly. It wasn't a coincidence of timing that had her climaxing the moment his beard had roughly caressed her cheek, his warm breath tickling her ear as he'd said what he probably thought was an insult, calling her his dirty little prize.

He'd called her *his*.

As far as wanting to break her? She was broken. How could he not see it? Wes had recognized it, exploited it, counted on it. She'd been broken over and over. She was accustomed to breaking and patching herself back together, only to be shattered once more. One day, she was sure the break would be permanent.

13

LIAR
Rogan

He spent days after the ceremony tormenting himself with his pet. He stayed home, stayed inside, presenting the image of a man enjoying his prize. When he wasn't with her or taking her with him, leading her by a leash, he would cuff her to his bed.

Torment, because other than the time he'd fucked her with his fingers, he hadn't touched her. Sexually, at least. It was a form of punishment, edging himself. He wanted to fuck her, but at the same time, he didn't want anything to do with her. So he fell into a routine, not unlike when he'd inherited Ruff.

He continued to watch her in the bathroom. She'd been mortified, silent tears coasting down her blazing-red cheeks, the first few times she had to take a shit in front of him. Like he cared, like he was bothered by it, judging her. He shat, too. He'd watched her with the same dissociation as he'd watched the dog. He was more annoyed by her cringing in horror than the bodily function; it was different from watching her pee. The power surge was still there, but it was dampened by her reaction, and he didn't understand it. He imagined she'd had to do the same in front of strangers.

Was it because she had to do it in front of him, specifically?

He couldn't ask. Well, he could, he supposed, but that would require her to answer.

Initially, after her morning piss, he tied her to the bed while he showered. He wasn't convinced that she wouldn't get the stupid idea in her head to run or stab him with his own kitchen knife. But soon, after he'd thought about their first day together, their time in the shower, one too many times, he'd decided he wanted her in the shower with him. He behaved more gentlemanly, heating the water before dragging her in with him.

He could keep an eye on her this way, he justified, not that he needed a justification. She was his. *His, his, his.* And he took pleasure from it, having her wash him. She gave him a hard-on every time. He marveled at his own discipline, especially now that he'd had a small taste of her and imagined going back for a direct delivery. The mental image he had of his face buried in her cunt, licking, lapping, and sucking, teased him. Again: torment.

During the day, she sat on her mat in the front room. She'd zone out, going inside herself. He couldn't blame her, though he couldn't bring himself to do anything for her. Maybe she was better off disappearing inside her mind.

She ate when he fed her. He put a bowl of water beside her mat; she'd given it a wary side-eye in response. He didn't care what she thought of it. When she was thirsty, she could drink; he didn't want to have to monitor her liquid intake.

Her output, however, he remained intrigued by.

He wasn't sure what he'd do with her when he went back to work. He'd need to go back soon. There were very few communications specialists on the island, so he would be needed. He was also a volunteer firefighter. Most men were; a few women, as well. In truth, they played at being firefighters. He had been a boy when the last fire had broken out on the island.

It was his knack for systems that had served him well, made him popular. The comms guys here—and they were all men—were treated like celebrities. That was why he was allowed to go to the mainland for classes. Technology was changing quickly, and in order to stay ahead and anticipate the needs of their community, he was given the opportunity to learn. Signal jamming, that sort of thing; whatever it took to keep their island from drawing too much interest while also meeting the connectivity needs of their guests and maintaining their anonymity.

He wanted to walk around knowing his every movement wasn't being monitored. He'd wanted that with Narlina.

Fucking traitorous bitch. Fucking liar.

Most residents were not given the privilege of leaving the island. Mainland assignments were reserved for the few who'd proven their loyalty. Of course, the tracking device ensured it. To his knowledge, no one had tried to run, be it an involuntary guest of the island or someone allowed mainland privileges. Though maybe they had, because the event would surely be covered up quickly and kept from the general population.

Wes visited the mainland, too. It had been a rare occasion when they were there at the same time. That's when Rogan had started planning, when they were away from the ears and eyes—and the listening devices he'd helped create—of the island.

Because he was responsible for tech, he knew how to circumvent it, get around it, redirect it. He'd been playing the long game for some time, because he'd had Narlina, and knowledge was power. They'd also needed privacy, places to plan. Places to fuck.

He suddenly had the desire to return to work. After a gifting, the recipient was given several days off from their tasks. The time had been provided so he could settle in with his prize—namely, to fuck the life out of her, present the rules, add to her training—though it wasn't needed. He wasn't fucking her, and he didn't know how to train her. He was itching to get to the comms room and pull tapes and video feed so he could try to puzzle out why Narlina had betrayed him.

Wes came by once more. When he saw her, complete with dog collar and water dish, he'd shaken his head. "She isn't actually a dog." He'd tilted his head. "The collar's hot, though."

Rogan ignored the reprimand, though he agreed with the observation. It was hotter when she was cuffed, but he didn't tell Wes that. His friend didn't need any more stimulation when it came to her, obsessed as he was. Through the entire visit, he begged to fuck her. Denying Wes became an unexpected source of empowerment. It wasn't meant to be cruel, but misery loves company.

Rogan couldn't fuck the woman he wanted, so Wes didn't get to fuck his obsession.

14

MANIPULATION
The Prize

She eyed the bowl of oatmeal Rogan had set in front of her with distaste. On this side of the veil, all of her horrors were revisiting her. One of those nightmares was oatmeal. What was a simple and quick meal for most was something far more sinister for her. She'd avoided it her entire adult life. Until now. In this moment, the nondescript bowl with the bland-looking mush triggered a flood of memories.

He watched her, looming over her, perhaps sensing her hesitation or noticing the look on her face. His breath was steady as hers increased. In any other situation, she would have knocked the bowl away, but she didn't know what that sort of rebellion would cost her here.

"Eat it," he huffed, annoyed. On the heels of his words, he turned and walked away, dismissing her and the turmoil he'd just unleashed.

"Eat it!"

Powerless and scared, she shook in her chair, watching her foster sibling eat the oatmeal into which the girl had just puked. The foster child raised a spoonful of vomitous gruel to her mouth, the utensil in her hand shaking hard, her reluctance evident. Was she hoping for disaster to strike and save her from this task?

It wouldn't. Nothing ever did. There would be no respite, no one to save them. She'd given up on that fantasy long ago.

Quivering lips opened to take in the vile concoction, tears falling in rivulets down her cheeks. The minute the spoon hit her mouth, she gagged. Swallowing, she trembled and fought to keep it down; failed. The vomit rose again, refilling her bowl.

"Please stop!" she'd once begged on behalf of a former foster brother, and herself, honestly. Her torment wasn't the same, but the guilt was a constant companion.

The sickly sweet response? "He's doing it on purpose. He likes it, otherwise he'd eat it and stop wasting food."

As an adult, she wondered if the food hadn't been laced with something to make them throw up. The sadistic performance brought immense pleasure; exorcizing demons through vulnerable children, becoming a monster in the process.

Being the victim of that abuse was unthinkable. Watching it happen, over and over, and not knowing how to stop it, how to provide relief, was soul-crushing. That was probably the point. Compared to the cries and screams from the basement—one episode so violent that it broke the belt buckle—the sickening breakfast was the lesser of evils.

In retrospect—or twisted cognition—she could label it as abuse. What had happened to her, however, was difficult to label. Being witness to the act was very different from being forced to eat vomit.

How long can a person dwell in anxiety, in fear, in torment? The answer: however long it takes to survive.

She left as soon as she could. Coercion and manipulation through money used to maintain her dependence had made it difficult. She had been determined to never find herself in a position to rely on anyone financially, and she'd persevered in that. Her life had been one of borderline poverty, but it had been a life she owned.

She didn't know what had become of the innocents who'd had the misfortune of being placed in her household. Some names she knew, others she didn't. Even after striking out on her own, the guilt that ate at her kept her from looking them up, kept her from apologizing, begging for forgiveness.

The few adults she'd told hadn't believed the wild stories. They'd assumed she was lying to get attention. Attention was the last thing she wanted. She only wanted relief. Every adult she encountered had failed her and made her question her own recollections.

"That can't be."

"That didn't happen. It couldn't happen."

"You're lying, aren't you?"

Threats existed everywhere; no one and nothing was safe. Yet, illogically, she had faith that someone would save her, and it fed her driving desire for affection. Acceptance. She was a contradiction: distrustful yet yearning. And therefore easily manipulated. Although she'd never call herself gullible, her need to believe in another—to be able to take that person at face value and not be disappointed by them—led her to exactly that. Promises made were broken. She was told what she wanted to hear so they could get out of her what they wanted.

Her ability to judge the intentions of others was skewed, which was how she found herself in relationships with people like Ann and Wes. Being taken advantage of repeatedly made her realize she couldn't trust her instincts. She didn't understand boundaries; a friendly person was a friend until their actions made it clear they weren't. It broke her heart every time. Then she'd dive into self-reflection and self-flagellation, obsessing over what it was about her that made her unworthy. She'd studied friendships between other people, convinced they were pretending while at the same time wanting the same connection. She was a good person who, once she was on her own, did what she could for the few people in her life. The pain that came with the disappointment was reminiscent of that which she'd experienced growing up; the rejection was too hot.

Eventually, she erred on the side of caution and tossed up walls, keeping her distance and shutting down feelings. Solitude was safe, a form of protection and self-preservation, although her soul screamed for love, for someone to believe in and to be believed in herself.

Not that she deserved it. And wasn't she pitiful for wanting it?

Yet she'd let her guard down when a pretty man smiled. She'd been so good at pushing others away that she became starved for affection, a connection. True to form, Wes disappointed her and left her to the mercy of others. One would think she would have learned, but that's not how a tortured mind like hers worked. She was prone to extremes. She was exhausted all the time. Constant vigilance against the danger, and the emotional toll of having a breakdown over the little things, wore her down.

But in her current situation, where all of her power had been taken from her, where decisions were made for her, she found relief. A weight had been lifted when she was ordered not to speak.

There was also the deep-seated hope that Wes actually cared about her. He could be wonderful; she had experienced it. He still retained that ability, right? And he'd chosen her to bring back for himself. *Her.*

It was fucked up to think that way, to need that from him, from them. But existing in fear, in terror, was as familiar to her as slipping into a favorite hoodie. This was a skin she knew how to wear. As horrifying as it might be, she was grateful someone else had taken control. Yes, she cried, was embarrassed, and yes, aroused, but she'd been crafted for this, manipulated into the type of person who perfectly fit the role of another's *prize*.

The oatmeal remained untouched. It grew cold and hard as time passed, even as her stomach growled. Breaking was a familiar pattern for her, but in this, she refused to bend.

15

FUCKING

Rogan

Did he care if she didn't want to eat? No. The untouched oatmeal remained beside her bed for two days, despite the way her stomach protested its emptiness. The rumblings had been audible; it had been his symphony at night. Her expression remained impassive, checked out. But she had zoned out before. This time, something was definitely going on inside her head. He just didn't care.

He threw the meal away when it started to stink. Her look of appreciation and relief when he took it away astonished him. She sagged back against the wall, as though all her physical strength had been sapped, like she'd been guarding against the meal. He ignored her reaction as he turned away from her.

With grateful expressions like that, he would be hard-pressed not to fuck her sooner rather than later. It was inevitable, he supposed, but he didn't want to break. He didn't *want* to want her, even to scratch an itch. It would humanize her more than the glimpses of personality that had broken through.

After cleaning out the bowl of uneaten oatmeal, he tossed her a cold, uncooked hot dog. She snatched it from the floor, hands shaking, and devoured it. Her wild eyes sought him out, fearful, as if he'd storm over and take it away before she could consume it. He wouldn't have had the chance. The processed meat was gone so quickly he wasn't sure she'd chewed.

If she was so hungry, why wouldn't she eat the oatmeal? It wasn't an allergy. He'd given her an oats and honey granola bar, and she'd had no issue. In order to satisfy his curiosity, he would need to speak to her; rather, she would need to answer. And that wasn't happening.

A tap on his door distracted him. It was Wes's specific knock. An instant later, the door opened and his sunshiny friend walked through. After he gave Rogan a brief smile, he turned his attention to the corner.

"Hey, Doll."

At the greeting, she shifted, curling herself further into the corner. When Ruff was younger, he'd retreat to his crate when he was tired or scared. This attempt to further retreat was reminiscent of that behavior.

"Still keeping her in the corner?" Wes's voice was full of reproach and disappointment. "Do you let her stand? Move around?"

Rogan gave him a hard stare.

"Fucking would be exercise, at least," Wes said drolly, approaching him in the kitchen. "If you'd let her off her leash"—he chuckled at his own joke—"she could clean for you. Or cook. She's pretty good at both."

Rogan regarded her again. She was listening, but her face was carefully turned away. He hadn't thought beyond his own misery to what skills she might have, what she could functionally contribute.

"Doll, get over here."

She tensed, and a guarded look came over her face. Was she expecting what happened the last time Wes had called her over to occur? Maybe something more? After all, she'd responded to *him*. And he could still remember the taste of her on his tongue when he'd licked his fingers clean.

Despite her obvious reluctance to answer Wes's call, she looked to Rogan, seeking permission to move. He nodded once. She flushed, but she moved quickly, scrambling to stand. Was it because she didn't want to be ordered to crawl?

She swayed a little when she was upright and pressed a hand to the wall to steady herself. Maybe Wes had a point; sitting in a corner all day wasn't good for her. Of course, she also hadn't eaten anything but a cold hot dog for two days. But what the fuck else was he going to do with her? How could he trust her in the apartment on her own, with plenty of tools of destruction at her disposal?

Her approach was hesitant, halting. This time, it wasn't because she was off balance. She kept her eyes on him, avoiding Wes.

"Here." Rogan pointed to the floor in front of him.

Now she did look at Wes, then back at Rogan. She'd caught on, that he was placing her between the two of them. Still, she followed his instructions. Her gaze bounced between them warily. But Wes said she could cook, so he'd see if that was true. Maybe she could serve a purpose.

She stopped in front of him and cast a concerned look over her shoulder. Then she focused on a spot on his neck. It irritated him, her refusal to look him in the eye. She had likely been instructed not to—something like looking a beast directly in the eyes; one wouldn't want to unintentionally challenge it. Even so, that didn't assuage his annoyance. He wouldn't take her to task on it right now. Instead, he grasped her shoulders and turned her toward Wes.

Wes smiled, taking his time in perusing her. His expression was full of lust, but there were also hints of wistfulness and regret. Wes didn't regret taking her. No, the regret was because he'd given her up. Rogan could offer her to him, but he was growing fond of the control.

"Doll." Wes chucked her under her chin. She flinched, but Wes didn't acknowledge it. "If we give you free rein of the kitchen, do you promise not to take a knife and try to stab us?" His tone was light, joking, but the question and concern were real.

She nodded.

"Good girl."

It wasn't enough. Rogan asked, "Do you promise not to use it on yourself?"

Wes frowned in disbelief at the question, but he quickly looked from Rogan to her for her answer.

It took a moment, but she nodded jerkily.

Reaching around, he cuffed her throat above the collar and jerked her head back. She stumbled against him.

Lowering his lips to her ear, he ground out, "You didn't answer fast enough, little prize." He squeezed once. "You belong to me. You aren't allowed to take anything away from me, including yourself. Got it?"

She was looking at the ceiling, her eyes watering and darting around as though she'd find answers written up there. But she nodded.

Before them, Wes was watching them with a small, knowing smile.

"What are you grinning about?"

Wes raised a pale brow. "I know she's supposed to cook, but..." He assessed her hungrily. "I'm in the mood for something sweet." His focus returned to Rogan. "If you'd just have a taste, man."

Rogan stilled, suddenly aware of her body heat pressed against him. He *had* tasted her, licking her from his fingers. He pressed on her throat, urging her head farther back against his shoulder.

Her attention flew to him, then away. Her breathing picked up. Fear? Or anticipation? Both?

"Oh, Doll," Wes breathed out. He took a step forward and cupped her breasts through the t-shirt, pinching and rolling her pebbled nipples.

She jerked and sucked in a breath.

Wes's eyes burned with desire, igniting a similar response in Rogan. That reaction was enough to have him caving. He'd been wanting her for days anyway. This way, he could blame his friend.

He still offered a slight protest, kept up the pretense. "She hasn't eaten."

Delight lit Wes's face. He lifted a hand to her chin, tilting her head back even farther. Rogan was now cheek-to-cheek with her, her backside flush against him.

"Then we'll fill her pretty little mouth, her stomach, with cum. We'll fill every part of her until she's bursting with us." Wes pressed himself to her, brushing his lips over hers. "You'd like that, wouldn't you, Doll?" Tilting his head slightly, he nipped lightly at Rogan's lips. "Let's make a mess."

Rogan breathed out, heart pounding and heat flooding his body. Yes, they should make a mess. He and Wes moved in unison, as though the moves were planned. He removed her shirt and moved his hands over her, brushing over Wes's roaming hands as he did the same. Rogan allowed himself to feel the pleasure elicited by the simple act. Finger-fucking didn't count. She'd had the shirt on, and he hadn't dallied. He reached around and grasped her breasts, burying his face in her neck, smelling the sweetness of her. Beyond the soap they used, her natural scent was detectable, and it was heady. "I fuck her first."

To his credit, Wes didn't point out that he'd had her before. Many times. Tonight, she was his new toy, and he would spill his cum inside her first. Wes liked a mess anyway; he'd revel in the sloppiness.

Because his hands were full of her breasts, Wes reached around her and tugged Rogan's pants down, freeing his cock. The sensation of his dick rebounding against her ass drove him wild. He wasn't sure where he wanted to plunge into her first. His dick didn't need any urging, but Wes grabbed him, jerking roughly. Rogan groaned, shuddering.

"Good to go," Wes chortled.

More than good. Fuck, he wasn't going to last long.

She was pliant in his hold, neither protesting nor participating. Her arms hung at her sides. Her breathing had increased, but panic could do that, too. She was leaning back against him, using him as support. Wes was before her, sucking a nipple as Rogan squeezed the soft tissue of her breast, holding it up in an offering to his friend's greedy mouth. True to form, he was sucking loudly, sloppily, licking, nipping.

Rogan took it in, the thrilling sight of his friend taking what was offered, then dragged his gaze up the slope of her chest and neck, to her profile. Her brow was pinched, lips turned down in... confusion? Uncertainty? Pain? If it was pain, it wasn't the physical kind; she wasn't being hurt in that way. Not yet.

But Rogan didn't want only a compliant body. He didn't want her to endure this, to endure him and Wes. He shouldn't have cared, but that didn't change what he needed. He couldn't take his pleasure unless there was something for her, even if he wasn't the one to deliver it.

He nipped at her jaw; she startled against him. His dick was snug in the crease of her ass, urging him to penetrate and take. But he didn't. Instead, he moved his mouth to her ear. He breathed against the lobe, taking it between his lips and tugging. His teeth slid from her skin, and he invited, "Take what we offer."

16

BOUNDARIES

The Prize

Take what they offer. The words weren't a demand; they were permission. They'd use her anyway, but those four words gave her a choice: *take*. Accept the use of her body, interpret it as adoration, take the opportunity to let go and slip into salaciousness instead of being an outsider watching her own ravishment. There was power in participation; she'd learned that. And she'd taken when he'd finger-fucked her. She'd daydreamed about him doing it to her again—doing more.

She could take it now, even if it was her former lover and deceiver who suckled her, shooting rivulets of pleasure through her. She'd loved him once, had loved how he touched her. And maybe it was wrong, but she loved his mouth on her now. Her body responded to his ministrations as it had before. He was familiar, a comfort, even. Memories of him and what he had done to her, for her, before this place, took over. All she had to do was portion off the part of her brain that accused him, was wounded by him.

It was easier than it should have been. His hot mouth and dedicated attention helped close the doors on those thoughts. Her nipples hardened further; her body was washed in heat. He wanted to please her body, and she wanted to be pleased.

She'd been given leave to let go, relieved of the burden of being their victim. Her tense muscles relaxed, and she lowered the guard she'd kept up against her own reactions, responses, and thrills. She was depraved to want this, she knew, but self-recrimination could wait. She wanted oblivion and mindlessness. She wanted to be loved, and if she couldn't have that, she'd settle for the illusion of it. By succumbing, she became more aware.

So she gave herself over to them. Wes lowered himself in front of her, kissing and licking as he went, and she caught her fingers in his hair. It was automatic. He gave her a cheeky grin in response, then angled forward and parted her slit with his tongue. He was ravenous for her, sloppy, tongue-fucking and sucking her with the ferocity of a man afraid his meal could be taken from him at any moment. She gasped, bouncing up on her toes and rocking her hips forward. The man behind her wrapped his arms around her, holding her in place. He moved slightly, sliding his cock along her backside.

She closed her eyes, concentrating only on sensation. Wes suckled and flicked her clit with his tongue. The heat of his mouth had her body flushing, her skin breaking out in goose bumps, and the wetness between her legs increased.

Feel, feel. Wes had been correct when he'd told Rogan that she'd wished for something like this. She hadn't wanted anything like that first night, forced to take Wes's cock until it choked her. That had been too reminiscent of her initial weeks here. But this? Two men surrounding her, their heat setting her body on fire, caressing her like she had value, their lips on her, their cocks hard and ready to take her. This was much closer to what she'd imagined.

She grasped Wes's hair, tugged. He moaned in response, the reverberations slicing through her and urging her hips to tilt toward him. In response to her not-so-subtle signal, he thrust his tongue inside her, lapping. The sounds of her arousal filled the air, her copious juices. He didn't stop, didn't slow, not for a long moment. After more swipes, licks, and sucks, his breath as hot as his tongue, he leaned back only a fraction. "She's ready for you."

The words didn't register until the man behind her tested her slickness with his fingers. *She's ready for you.* Yes, she was. In the deepest recesses of her mind, she'd been anticipating the moment when her owner claimed her fully. Instead of an angry demand that she yield to him, he was spreading her with two fingers, gauging the truth in Wes's words. She shivered.

His hand disappeared, only to be replaced with the crown of his cock. She held her breath as he slowly pushed into her. Below her, Wes watched his friend penetrate her, his expression wicked and satisfied. He bit his bottom lip, raising a brow as the man behind her filled her completely.

"Oh, fuck," her owner rasped in her ear. His fingers were on her hips, dipping into her flesh.

Wes caressed where they were joined. "Fucking beautiful. Her pussy is goddamn beautiful taking your cock."

Wes slid his hand farther back, beyond where she and Rogan were joined. Whatever he did, it made Rogan shudder and groan. He buried his face in her neck again, clearly affected. The tickle of his breath and beard made her shiver.

With another moan, Rogan moved inside her. Slow, long strokes like he was savoring the feel, the stretch of her, around him. His cock inside her swamped her with just as much desire as Wes's hand caressing their connection.

Rogan picked up the pace. Unsteady, she released Wes's hair and bent, grasping his shoulders. It opened her up more for her partner behind her, and it urged him on. He pistoned his hips faster, harder. Her breasts bounced with the movement.

Through half-lidded, desire-glazed eyes, she watched Wes. His lips were parted, and there was wonderment in his light irises. He was enthralled, turned on. Sweat had formed on his forehead, as it likely had on hers. Her legs trembled when Rogan hit an especially sweet spot.

Wes placed one hand on her abdomen, pressing lightly, and instantly, each of her nerves sang with an intense pleasure. He leaned forward and flicked her clit with his tongue urgently. She cried out, then choked off the sound.

Her brain filled, her vision blurred. The sound of Rogan's hips slamming into her ass reverberated, mingling with moans, groans, and Wes's loud sucking. She trembled even more, becoming utterly defeated, giving herself over to them and the crash of delightful delirium.

Then it happened. Sight, sound, and smell were suspended. Her brain and body exploded, and she was free of this place, from them. She found her wings and soared away, propelled to dizzying heights. She wanted to stay here, in her oblivious bliss, where she was warm and safe.

All too soon, though, she was tumbling back to earth, to reality, into the arms of the man who owned her.

Her head still spinning, she vaguely registered that she was being shifted. She let her head fall back on Rogan's shoulder. He was no longer inside her, but he was holding her up. Wes was standing in front of her, then he was pushing into her where Rogan had just been. Hot liquid seeped down her thighs, a gush forced out by Wes's cock.

"Doll, Doll, baby doll," Wes chanted as he buried himself inside her. He had no control, no patience or finesse. He rammed into her with desperate fury. "Fuck, Ro." He grasped his friend's hair.

In response, Rogan wrapped one arm around Wes, his other still supporting her weight. She, too, was embracing Wes, holding on as he drove into her. His thrusts were so deep, she raised on her tiptoes to relieve the pain. But this was pain she liked. She reveled in the stretch, the furious glide of flesh within flesh. Too soon, he tensed against her, his muscles shaking. He'd clamped his jaw shut, a strangled sound leaving him, as though he was attempting solidarity with her by orgasming in near silence.

For several minutes, the three of them remained where they were, catching their breaths. More hot liquid made its way down her thighs when Wes withdrew. He kissed her fiercely, his tongue swiping hers.

When he released her, his attention shifted behind her, and a devilish grin split his face. "I don't think we're messy enough."

The rumble of Rogan's laugh warmed her. She allowed herself a moment of contentment between them, and then his words registered.

They weren't finished with her.

Excitement shot through her, and her stupid heart leaped with hope.

· · · · ● · ● · · ·

Managing her expectations after this would be impossible. Despite the reminders her brain had given her, she chose to interpret the physical sensations they'd evoked as genuine affection. The sex continued for hours and in so many positions. She'd felt like a marionette, their bendable doll, and she reveled in it. She'd been as lost in desire as they were. And, blessedly, she'd taken the flight into nothingness a couple more times. When her stomach growled, Wes fed her, casting an accusatory look at his friend.

It didn't halt the fucking. While she nibbled on a sandwich, Wes and Rogan strong-armed each other, each vying for the upper hand. Wes gained it and drove himself into Rogan's ass. She suspected, however, that Rogan had thrown the game to appease Wes's irritation over his not feeding her. They were rough with one another. Far rougher than they were with her. In contrast, the way they treated her was almost tender.

That revelation hit at the exact moment Wes came. Rogan, in response, grabbed her while she was swallowing her food, unmindful that he'd nearly choked her with the suddenness of his movements. He'd plunged into her, thrusting one, two, three times before he released into her. She'd still been holding her sandwich.

Today, she was sore everywhere, even after sleeping in the bed. If she thought she'd slept well her first night with him, it was nothing compared to the deep, exhausted sleep she'd fallen into while snuggled between the two men.

They would disappoint her. She *knew* that, yet her heart urged her to think differently, urged her to ignore the fact that everyone she'd ever encountered had let her down. Desperation, deprivation, hope, and devastation. It was a cycle to which she was accustomed.

The sex hadn't been off-putting. It had been the opposite, in fact. It was touch, and it felt good. Sex could feel bad; she'd learned that as a child. But even the cruelest of touches fed hope. If she was good, if she pretended she liked it, her tormentor might reward her with affection after the physical pain had ended. Tenderness after the shredding, cajoling before. Endure one to receive the other. Hope for a reprieve, for her assaulters to be moved to saving her.

They never did. Moments after she provided what they'd needed, she was rejected. Rogan and Wes would reject her, too. Just like her parents, her so-called friends, her dubious suitors, then Wes. Eventually, they would turn away from her. Why wouldn't they? Fundamentally, she was lacking, faulty. And that led others to subject her to a nightmarish existence. Blind eyes were turned when depraved men feasted on a child.

Neither Rogan nor Wes truly cared about her. Wes had proven that by kidnapping her and turning her over, fully aware that she'd endure weeks of torture and torment, rape. At least, thanks to those other deplorable men, the practice hadn't been unfamiliar. Not that it was a competition, which experience was better or worse, then or now. Though to be subjected to it again after she'd gained her autonomy, her independence, was devastating. She'd thought she was wiser, more guarded. Was certain she could pick out the predators, refused to ever again be prey. After all, she knew better.

It turned out she was the same lost lamb led to slaughter. Age didn't matter. Awareness hadn't prepared her or protected her from it. She'd fallen in love. But he'd only seen her as a mark. She served a purpose with her body; the ease with which they'd shared her made it obvious she wasn't the first woman to have them both.

But her silly, stupid heart tripped over itself as that ridiculous thought wormed its way into her mind again. Wes had chosen her. *Her.* Out of everyone he had taken—this time or before—she was the one he'd wanted to keep for himself.

She would give herself whiplash ruminating on it.

They hated her.

They cared about her. At least, Wes did; Rogan enjoyed fucking her, though that was knowledge she could cling to.

These were equal truths in her brain, damaged and shaped by people worse than these two.

At least they hadn't drugged her. That thought hadn't hit her, shocked her, until the quiet hours of the night. Drugs assisted with compliance, obedience, and acquiescence. But she hadn't been subject to it or provided it. Her punishment, as it were, was to be wholly conscious and aware of every pang to want to belong. Once the caresses and the good feelings started to replace the constant boredom and fear, she'd have opted for blurry oblivion.

17

WHORE

Rogan

Fucking her was addicting. The seal, as it were, had been broken. Smashed. For as much as he hated her, he couldn't keep his dick out of her. In return, she'd wrap around him, clinging, bending to him like he was her salvation instead of her ruin. She had an expiration date; she had to know that as keenly as he did. Therefore, he fucked her like he was racing to get as much of her as he could before her time was up, knowing all the while that he would be the one to decide it.

He fucked her in his bed, in the shower, any time he felt like it. Since that first night with Wes and her, he'd kept her in his bed—cuffed, of course. She was a goddamn vision, cuffed, collared, and naked. Vulnerable to him, laid out like a buffet of sin. He could eat her, fuck her from any angle, or—his favorite nighttime ritual—edge her to the brink, then deny her. She couldn't beg for relief, she was helpless. He'd lick her tears away as he jerked himself off over her.

Knowing she was beside him, her pussy swollen and dripping, in physical torment for him, made him sleep like a fucking baby. If he was feeling merciful, he'd slap her clit with his belt. Fuck, it was enthralling to watch her orgasm through the pain, her expression conflicted. Before she'd come down from the high, he would be inside her.

Losing himself in her soft body, plunging into the sweet tightness of her, transported him. For those minutes, he could convince himself that he wasn't still on this island. Even so, it didn't stop him from berating her, degrading her, blaming her, as he pounded into her. Her tears from his games weren't enough.

"I resent your fear. I resent the air you breathe. I resent your beautiful face, your tight pussy." The words he slammed into her were as hard as his dick. She twisted and writhed beneath him as though getting off on the verbal lashings. "My prize. My little prize with this tight cunt. Are you worth it?"

His words propelled her, fueled her. She arched against him, seeking release. He tried not to enjoy this—her—until his mind blanked and he found his freedom inside her. But even as he cried out, clasping her close, he hated her.

He hated her because he *was* her. He was owned as much as she was, only his bindings were invisible. Her mere existence was a taunting reminder. No amount of fucking her would change that truth.

When Wes joined them, he wouldn't let his doll twist for long after Rogan edged, then denied her. He'd cast a disapproving look his way, then suck her clit. And that's all it would take. Her body would jolt like a live wire as she was given her release. With her restrained wrists and hard, peaked nipples, she was exquisite as she bucked and gasped, all while Wes remained between her legs, making sloppy noises.

Rogan was entranced by her; fascinated, really. He'd sat against the headboard one evening, stroking himself while watching his friend fuck her tits. She arched beneath him, her head dropping back. The sensual arc of her body had made him pump harder. With her unshackled hands gripping Wes's thighs, she'd tossed her head until her glazed gaze locked on his.

That's when it struck him: he'd never lay a hand on Narlina again, wouldn't allow himself to take comfort from the woman who'd betrayed him. But his prize was—and had been—taking pleasure from the man who'd betrayed her. Choice or not, her responses were real. Despite the horrors she must have endured, she allowed herself to be seduced by the man who'd delivered her to those horrors.

At that moment, he was hit with the urgent need to be inside her. He shoved Wes off and ripped her up from her prone position. Then, stretched out beneath her, he pulled her over his hips and drove up into her wet pussy with all his strength. Her tits bounced with the force of his thrusts. Fucking glorious sight: her peering down at him, her hands braced on his chest, as she rode him.

"Can I have her mouth?" Wes asked.

"No." Rogan wanted to study the face of the woman who could overcome, who could forgive the atrocities done to her in order to take want she needed. That was a gift, a power. And he wanted some of it. So he barreled into her, shoving her knees farther apart, getting as deep as he could. His cock was the conduit, siphoning that strength from her, taking from her. "She's my whore."

"Our whore," Wes argued. "If I can't have her mouth, then I'm taking her pussy, too."

She let out a squeak when Wes shoved her forward, forcing her to lie across Rogan's chest. Rogan stilled, his heart hammering. She pressed her hands to his chest and lifted slightly, her widened eyes searching his, wild and confused with fear and pain as Wes's cock nudged his own at her entrance.

There was a sharp slap, and she jumped.

"Relax!" Wes ordered.

It made her tense even more, nearly squeezing his dick off. "It'll hurt worse if you don't relax. Up to you. I'm coming in anyway."

Her face contorted in agony as Wes worked his way inside her; Rogan tried not to let his eyes roll back at the fucking awesome feeling of her pussy constricting while Wes's cock slid along his own, popping out more than once to smack his balls.

"Fuck," Rogan gasped. He'd broken a sweat, lying still while his best friend's dick fought to make its way into her. He wanted to fuck; his instinct was to thrust.

She dropped her head onto his shoulder, stifling sounds of discomfort. Her fingernails dug into his biceps. The sensation was mind-altering.

Two more strikes against flesh rang out when she wriggled. Hot droplets hit his neck. She was crying. It didn't matter. He wanted this, too. "We're taking this, pet. Let him in."

Her breaths a staccato rhythm, she fell limply against him, her hardened nipples searing his chest. Despite the pain, she was aroused.

His cock grew impossibly hard as Wes triumphed, his friend's dick dragging against his own sensitive flesh. "Goddamn. Fuck."

Wes chuckled. "Heaven is what this is."

Slowly, Wes withdrew before pushing back in. Loosening her. The tight fit and the friction were nirvana. Wes eased himself in and out a few times, coating his cock in her arousal—which soaked them both.

"That's a good girl, baby doll."

At the praise, she shivered in Rogan's arms. Rogan didn't have the wherewithal to consider why; he didn't care that she got off on the praise. Not when he could get her off with humiliation. And at this moment, he could only focus on not being the first to come as Wes started thrusting with purpose, the rubbing against his cock making him dizzy.

"Look at me," Rogan ordered.

Wes croaked out a laugh. "I am. Can't miss looking at your pretty face." He was over them on his knees, one arm braced to hold himself up.

"Not you." He grabbed a handful of her hair, tugging, forcing her to look at him.

A surge of pride and satisfaction ran through him at the sight of her desire-heavy lids, her dilated pupils, her flushed cheeks. She was taking in short breaths. She might be in pain, but she was getting off anyway, finding the pleasure in it.

Wes's rocking forced her clit against him, making him more determined not to be the first to detonate. He wanted to feel her explosion first, the way it would squeeze him and Wes simultaneously. The sweat on her face matched his own, matched Wes's. The sweat between their bodies enhanced the sensations, magnifying them. They were a grunting, moaning, twitching pile of limbs, the three of them connected.

For the first time since she'd landed at his feet, he wasn't angry. It didn't mean he wouldn't continue to berate and blame her. But feeling her come apart as both men were inside her made him soar.

Afterward, Wes had tenderly overseen her bath. Rogan had stood in the doorway. She wore a confused frown, as if she were perplexed by the care; worried, almost. But when Wes would lean in to kiss her, she responded.

Yeah, fucking her was easy when she bent to their demands so easily.

18

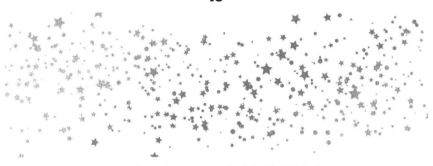

DISSOCIATION
The Prize

How did she do it? Compartmentalize what she'd suffered so she could revel in their touches, accept their cocks and kisses?

She could do it because she had been preconditioned to be loyal beyond abuse. Rogan was better to her than anyone—those few weeks with Wes excluded—despite the words he rained down on her. His resentment of her? His cruelty and reward from the belt? She'd take it, because it came with his protection. He was just as loyal to her because of his anger. When he fucked her, even as he said those things, she was his. Those words were for her. That was *her* prize, little treasures she could tuck away.

He gave her these little treats—his loyalty, affection, and protection—and she would return it all tenfold. Her heart had an enormous capacity to forgive the most awful, egregious atrocities and give love in return. Crave love.

It shouldn't make sense. But a desperately lonely and neglected heart had the capacity to do many things.

She'd watched a documentary once about pit bulls and how they had copious amounts of love and loyalty in them. That loyalty was what led them into the pits to tear each other to pieces or be torn up, even killed; their loving and loyal natures were used against them. It was cruel beyond comprehension. After, if they survived the fights, their goofy faces would be full of love for their masters, their tormentors. The existence of such cruelty was heartbreaking, yet these resilient dogs came through with love in their hearts.

Did she find it ironic that she had compared herself to pit bulls as she sat on a dog's bed? Should she be thankful that she didn't have to tear anyone else apart for survival? Though she shouldn't get ahead of herself. After all she'd seen and endured, that wasn't out of the realm of possibility. She could have done it, not for anyone else, but for her own survival. It was one of those thoughts she turned away from; a truth so dark she ignored it.

Her upbringing had resembled that type of scenario in some ways. She had been an innocent creature who spent her childhood terrified one minute and expected to love unconditionally the next. Even if it was impossible for that love to be unconditional. Not when it was forced, a learned behavior. She'd survived it, endured it. She'd learned to stay quiet, stay small, provide the emotion—or lack thereof—expected of her. She had witnessed horrors, then assured the person who created her nightmares that they were loved. Forgiven. Absolved.

While the circumstances weren't the same, her status—helpless and determined to survive—was. She'd had no power then, and she had no power now. Her only power came in her will and her strength. She hadn't suffered her past only to succumb to this. Even if there had been days when the drive to give up overwhelmed her.

How could she desire Wes? Because she always had. She'd shared with him the fantasy of being completely submissive, at his mercy, and he'd brought her here. He had fulfilled her wish in the cruelest and darkest manner. But she repeated to herself: *he chose me, he chose me.*

Rogan was easier to want. His circumstance mirrored her own. His hatred was passion. He felt something for her, which was better than indifference. His attention, although too close at times—like when she had to use the bathroom—was still attention.

In the most toxic, twisted way, these men filled emotional holes. So she would take what they offered, as Rogan had induced, and not dwell on the future. There would be no point. She didn't have one. Instead, she focused on the immediate, existing in the moment. She took from them when they came for her, delighting her body with their mouths, hands, and cocks. They were equally delighted when she rubbed their cocks together, her mouth devouring them at the same time. She was intrigued when their cocks satisfied each other, too.

Wes and Rogan's rough play and fucking were new for her, their complete openness and abandon. It was thrilling to watch during the rare instances she wasn't included. One occasion, when she was left out, Wes had shoved Rogan against the refrigerator as they argued, holding him there with his arm spanning Rogan's clavicle, and jerked him off. Rogan had cursed and twisted, but he didn't break away. After he came all over both men, Wes had pulled him in and hugged him, murmuring words that had been lost to her.

Their brutality, their crudeness with one another, riveted and excited her. So, yes, when they turned that on her, drawing out her orgasms with brutish cruelty, she maintained her loyalty, would continue to do so, because she knew how to walk out of the ring and love her abuser.

It was all the more easier here, because she didn't feel abused by them.

19

GAUNTLET

Rogan

The silence was maddening. Being cooped up in the apartment more so. His pet shifted on her bed, her gaze listless, a visual representation of how he felt. When he—they—weren't fucking her, and when she wasn't preparing the occasional meal, she sat blankly in her corner.

Watching her made him restless. He needed air.

He retrieved a pair of cut-off sweatpants for her. These in particular had a drawstring at the waist that would keep them on her hips. Though the leggings hadn't been a deterrent on the walk to the clinic, they had slowed any wandering hands, giving him the opportunity to intervene. As he approached her, he held them out. She didn't immediately reach for the article. Instead, she regarded him, brows slightly lowered in question.

Dropping the article, he ordered, "Put them on. We're going out."

At the door, he took her leash off its hook. Though his back was to her, he sensed her silent approach, the air shifting, the scent of her wrapping around him. When he ducked his head and looked back, she jerked to a halt, as though she was doing something wrong.

He pointed to a spot on the ground in front of him. "Here."

She hustled around him to stand with her back to the door, facing him. Her silent regard was louder than any words she could have spoken. She watched him for cues, read him, as if making sure he was catered to. It stroked his ego, even as it was disconcerting. To distract himself from the intensity of her attention, he considered the clothes she wore: another of his t-shirts and the shorts. Both were baggy on her, but she still looked fucking spectacular. Inviting.

He heeded her body's summons, circling her neck with his free hand and pressing her against the door, then holding her there with his own. Her eyes widened at the suddenness of his movement, but she relaxed into his hold, his touch, almost instantly, still in tune to him. Her response was heady, the trust implicit. His dick stiffened.

He let out a low growl at the reaction. If he started fucking her now, they wouldn't leave the apartment. The sight of her big brown eyes watching him from her pale face leveled him out. He bit her bottom lip, committing to rewarding himself for the outing—the sunlight and fresh air—later. Once they returned, he'd make her ride his face until she came.

Stepping back, he clicked the leash onto the collar. Her body twitched in response. Was it the break in their connection that startled her, or something deeper within that rebelled against the leash?

It didn't matter. He took another step away from her luscious body, jerking on the tether. She stumbled forward, away from the door. He pulled it open in the next second, still battling his lust despite his resolve.

He would go to the water, the beach. The mainland could be seen from there. He was homesick for a place he barely knew. A place where he hadn't grown up. Other islands dotted the ocean, but the mainland had held his attention since he'd experienced what life could be. As a kid, he hadn't paid much attention to their tutor beyond the tales they were told about the evils of the place, the monsters inhabiting it.

Irony at its finest.

A few people called out in greeting as he led his pet. To his relief, those who passed by them merely looked at her. They were still curious—let them be—but no one touched her.

The sandy beaches that surrounded the island were broken up by volcanic rocks. There was a cliff on the opposite side, lending grandeur to the bungalows there. In his lifetime, several people had leaped from the heights to their peril. He glanced askance at his prize, determined to keep her from learning of them.

They were at the water's edge, gentle waves licking their bare feet, then dashing away again. The surf could be heard in the distance above the wind, but the water teasing their toes was part of the shallows, calmer.

A small smile lit her face. It was so slight, he wasn't sure he wasn't imagining it.

He made a show of letting go of her leash, letting it dangle down the front of her, between her breasts. "Go ahead. Swim."

She lifted her face, directing her attention from her toes to the ocean in front of her. Her expression lightened, looked hopeful, even. But after a moment, she grew still, her gaze fixed. She had spotted the distant land. He could guess her thoughts, because he'd had them himself: so close. Freedom was so close. Her longing matched his. For the space of a few breaths, he allowed himself to feel the connection to her, a bond they shared.

"Hey-yo, Rogan!"

At the sound of his name, he looked over his shoulder.

Larry was walking toward them. The older man called out to Rogan again, but his focus was on her.

Rogan nudged her arm. "Go on. Swim."

In his periphery, she side-eyed him for a second. Then she glanced over her shoulder. One look at the man ogling her, and she headed into the water. The sound that escaped her as the water lapped over her ankles sounded like relief. She had no idea. Even for this place, Larry was loathsome. It came as no surprise that he was Alan's right-hand man. And chief ass-kisser.

Turning, Rogan walked back up the sand to intercept—although he listened for the splashing that indicated she was in the water—and block. "Larry. What can I do for you?"

Larry shifted to one side, casting his attention beyond Rogan. His question was asked on a snicker. "How are you adjusting?"

Rather than telling him the truth—that winning a human being was his worst nightmare, especially when it was in place of love and liberation from this place—he side-stepped, attempting once more to block the other man's view. "The glitter paint was a bitch to clean up." It was a safe response. And true.

"Noted." His attention hadn't wandered from the prey in his sights. "When will you be ready to bring her out to play?"

Never. He'd witnessed the way Larry treated his slaves. Rogan might not have wanted his prize, but he sure as shit wouldn't let this creepy prick have a go at her. He had always been uneasy around the man, even as a child. Until this moment, he'd been able to handle his innate dislike. Now, the sleazy man brought out his protective side.

He had never let Larry pet Ruff, either.

"She's playing," he answered.

Larry finally looked from the water to him, assessing in a calculated way that made Rogan's stomach clench. This man had the authority to demand Rogan hand her over. Hell, he could demand Rogan bend over. They were owned, all of them. The leash just looked different.

"In your selfish phase still?"

Rogan glanced away. For fuck's sake.

"We'll see."

It took all of his willpower not to clench his fists or jaw, not to glare in warning at the man. He could guess at the meaning behind the question. Larry wanted his turn, but he'd approach it—how to phrase it?—diplomatically.

Rogan's unease turned into trepidation. Because Larry saw a victim he could torture without reprimand. There were only three men who wielded this kind of power: Alan, Trent, and Larry. But although he had the power, Trent never used it against them.

After they'd stared one another down for another few seconds, Larry looked back toward the ocean and tipped his head forward in a quick nod. "Better let her know about the sharks."

At first, Rogan interpreted it as a warning about Larry himself: yes, Larry was a shark. Larry had professed it more than once, and there was that quote Rogan heard on the mainland: when someone tells you who they are, believe them. The thought cycled quickly before realization dawned on him. He looked over his shoulder, and his stomach sank. "Holy shit." The distance she'd achieved made it look like she'd walked straight into the water and started swimming toward the mainland. Without hesitation, he ran into the water, splashing sloppily. Larry's laugh followed him on the wind.

As soon as he was deep enough, he dove, swimming toward her with the same determination she was using to swim away. The sharks were real enough, Larry aside, but what was more alarming was the sudden pull and spit out into the current that would have her at sea as soon as she cleared the calmer waves.

"Prize!" He doubted she could hear him over the waves and wind and what was most likely her pounding heart. His heartbeat was deafening.

Shouting took too much effort anyway. So he locked on her and allowed the adrenaline to spur him along. For every kick and stroke he took toward her, he swore she took ten; he wasn't closing the distance fast enough.

And then, all of a sudden, there she was, her legs and arms moving with singular focus, her strokes clean. It gave him a glimpse of who she was, or at least what she could do. And she could swim; was a strong swimmer, in fact.

Grasping her ankle, he yanked her back toward him. She screamed, taking in a mouthful of water in the process. As she coughed and choked on the water, she fought back.

But he eventually restrained her, wrapping his arm around her waist, holding her against him, her back to his chest. "Stop it! There are sharks. Quit fucking splashing."

The splashing ceased, but she continued to wriggle in his arms, trying to get away.

"And that's the current up ahead. Besides, the land is a mirage; it isn't that close. It's miles away. You'd never make it. Many others have tried." He fucking knew how unattainable the mainland was, even while it was in sight.

Bobbing in the water, he grabbed a fistful of her hair and yanked her head to his shoulder so he could glare at her. They kicked together to stay afloat, their legs sliding against each other's. Her fingers dug into his arm around her waist, but she no longer fought him. Her expression of devastation echoed his own sentiment. He couldn't blame her for making a break for it, but at the same time, it wasn't the best thought-out plan.

"Are you trying to steal from me?"

Her gaze slowly moved to his, her lips turned down in an uncertain frown.

"Taking yourself away means you're stealing from me. *No one* steals from me." The words echoed his earlier warning. The time she had been too slow to respond about the knives.

Tears gathered in her eyes and her bottom lip quivered.

"Are you ready to go back?" It was rhetorical. He wasn't actually giving her the option of continuing her journey toward death or returning with him. They were both exhausted and farther away from the shoreline than he was comfortable with.

He snagged her sopping leash and made for the shore. When she lagged beside him, he tugged her along. From her sluggish movements, it was clear she wasn't fighting him or trying to be difficult. She'd just spent all her energy on her mad dash, and now she was waning.

Eventually, the sand rose up beneath them, and they could stand. Both breathing heavily, they staggered onto the beach. He was relieved Larry had fucked off instead of remaining to watch him chase down his runaway.

"Fuck," he breathed out. His clothes were heavy, his white shirt clinging to her, detailing her breasts and hardened nipples. The shorts were gone. She'd probably discarded them when they'd gotten heavy.

She stood meekly an arm's length away, gingerly wringing out her hair, stealing glances at him. Dropping his head back, he surveyed the clear blue sky. Punishment was warranted for her stunt. Having her sit on his face when they returned wasn't punitive. A flare of resentment swept over him. Damn her for putting him in this position.

As he righted himself, he caught sight of brilliant blue: Narlina. Fuck him. He nearly collapsed, overwhelmed. The only thing keeping him on his feet was her husband standing beside her. They looked like they were merely strolling on the upper path, as they would any day, but Rogan suspected this particular outing had been encouraged by Larry.

The couple paused, looking like mismatched chairs. Elegant, youthful beauty next to a maturing effete man without an ounce of good looks. He'd never been handsome, nor would he ever be.

There were no greetings or calls of acknowledgment; they would have to yell to be heard, and it wouldn't have been dignified. Narlina's eyes bounced between him and the woman behind him. Alan, however, was fixated on the prize, his regard of the sopping wet woman thorough, full of interest. A nearly naked woman with a white t-shirt clinging to her curves was a pleasant sight for anyone, but his pet was especially breathtaking.

For the second time that day, Rogan shifted his stance to block her from the view of a predator. It drew both sets of eyes to him. Narlina narrowed hers. Alan studied with cruel curiosity.

Rogan barely breathed. A threat danced in the air between them. Pushing down his sense of doom, Rogan tipped his head politely. The gesture was belated, but it provided everyone an excuse to break the tension.

Still glaring, Narlina caressed her husband's arm, drawing his attention away. She angled closer, as if murmuring to him. Alan stared hard enough that Rogan was reasonably certain the scene was emblazoned on the man's memory.

Abruptly, Alan turned. He took his wife by her elbow and quickly guided her in the direction from which they'd come, furthering Rogan's suspicion that the encounter had been designed.

Narlina cast a final look over her shoulder, her expression a violent mix of envy and anger, the promise of revenge in her eyes, as if she had a right to be vengeful.

20

FAWN
The Prize

Her tears fell unheeded. Rogan's hand met her bare ass harshly, blow after blow, so many times the sensations transformed from stinging pain to hot to bordering on numbness. With the force he was using, his hand had to be experiencing the same. She attempted to remain stoic, and she succeeded during the initial strikes, but eventually her overwhelmed senses and devastation brought on the tears. She grieved her loss, using the punishment as an excuse to let her mask slip and release the emotion.

She was draped over his raised thigh, his foot braced on the kitchen chair. Her damp shirt was up, her ass bare. She'd removed the shorts early on when she was in the water because they'd become waterlogged.

The spanking was deserved. Her actions had been reckless. He'd saved her from her desperation and idiocy. But she'd seen land, and he had been preoccupied. Once she started walking, she kept going, and then she was swimming. Had she honestly thought she could make it? She didn't know. She hadn't analyzed her actions; she'd simply struck out.

She'd blame her momentary loss of sanity on sensory overload. After spending weeks in a cage, then being sequestered in the apartment, the cloudless sky, warm breezes, smell of the ocean, and the feel of the sand beneath her feet had overpowered her. Their walk to the clinic had been fraught with fear and full of grabbing hands and uncertainty. Like that day, the weather today was pleasant, beautiful. She appreciated it more than she ever had before. The rare treat had lured her into thinking there was possibility, and optimism had run through her.

Until she'd felt his hand on her ankle, dragging her back toward him, nothing existed but that distant land and her single-minded drive to reach it. His rebuke was confusing. He hated her, so why not let her go, let her wash away? Because then he'd lose a possession?

Everything about his actions confused her. Stopping her, dragging her back—sometimes by tugging on the leash because she was exhausted and defeated—and his subtle shift in stance once they'd returned to the beach.

Rogan's spiked vigilance and tenseness were palpable as he stared at the woman she'd seen that day in the arena. She'd paid little mind to the couple watching them other than to note that it was the same woman. As soon as Rogan blocked her, she tuned in to him and his wariness. Her exhaustion left her no other choice; she could only concentrate on one thing, and he was her world.

Even now, as he slammed his palm against her ass, she tuned in to him and the corporal punishment he dealt, letting it ground her. It pulled her from anguish and allowed her to focus on the pain. There was peace in it.

Eventually, her quiet sobs tapered off, leaving her soul blessedly numb.

Her tears ceased altogether by the time he stopped. Her exhaustion was complete. Based on the sounds of his breath, so was his. The hand that had provided punishment now soothed. He caressed her ass, tracing over what she knew had to be red welts, because she was sensitive to his touch. The lack of feeling was short-lived. His touch now elicited a stinging sensation entwined with tingles of pleasure.

When he dipped a finger, he found her wet. She couldn't control her arousal any more than she could the waves that had teased her toes. As quickly as he'd explored, his fingers retreated. She bit her lip to keep from protesting the loss.

With a hand cuffed around her nape, he pulled her up. She stumbled against him, dizzy, as the blood rushed out of her head.

His grip tightened, steadying her. "Will you do that again, pet?"

She was quick to shake her head in assurance. By now she understood that hesitation on her part would be met with more discipline. Although her body wasn't opposed to how he liked to reprimand her most of the time.

Timely response or not, he continued his punishment. In a quick maneuver, he had her lying on the table while he took his seat between her legs. She was instantly wetter, already anticipating his next move. He grasped her thighs and pulled her toward him. With her arms lax beside her, she went pliant, glad for the reprieve. Despite the pounding of her clit, begging for relief, she was balancing on the edge of sleep.

But the moment he plunged his tongue into her, her body lit up, exhaustion forgotten. He kissed her, licked her, using his thumbs to spread her lips, massaging in a circular motion. She arched, her mouth open in a silent plea. Her muscles clenched as she sought her release. The multitude of sensations created a single-mindedness in her not unlike when she'd struck out for the mainland. It was madness, instinct, and desperation.

While his thumbs tucked, caressed, and teased, he gripped her sore ass cheeks, dragging his nails along her flesh. It confused her brain, this pleasure scored with pain. And she loved it, the conflicting sensitivities. She pressed her calves into his shoulders to lift herself to him, chasing relief.

In response, Rogan lifted his head.

Instantly, her desire increased, and she gripped the edges of the table to stop herself from curling her fingers in his hair and returning him to his task. A whimper of distress left her. Her muscles quaked as she stared at the ceiling, willing him to continue so her speeding mind could find its calm in the aftermath of the glorious storm.

"Stay still."

It was a near impossible order, not that she had any choice but to adhere. Her flesh was in flames. It enhanced the soreness of her reddened ass, her blood racing through her veins contributing to the throbbing. Pleasure danced with pain, short-circuiting her besieged brain.

Burying his face again, he attacked her clit, flicking and sucking. He slipped his thumbs inside her. The enticing action had her digging her fingernails into the wood. *There, there, there.* Her mind slipped toward the blessed oblivion, her body teetering on the precipice that would tip her into the welcome, white void.

Rogan lurched to his feet, shoving her legs farther apart as he stood over her. Then he released his hold on her. His movement tore a breathy sob from her lungs. He denied her at the brink, at the edge of mental and physical annihilation; a promise broken. She shivered from the need to explode, to seek refuge in the mindlessness. Tears welled in her eyes again. She wriggled in an effort to find friction so she could finish herself off, but with her legs apart and her arms out, there was nothing but the devastatingly empty air.

"Stay still." The command was issued on a low growl this time, his voice strained. He grasped her ankles and placed her feet on the table, his hard look an addition to his spoken words to leave her legs spread.

Still looming above her, he took his cock out. Hot tears blurred her vision and streamed down the sides of her face as he glowered at her, all the while working himself. She wanted—craved, needed—him to move closer, to touch her or plunge into her. A full-body shiver overtook her.

He came, a prolonged low hum escaping him as he did. His dark eyes were on hers, feral and angry. His cum hit her stomach, abdomen, and pussy, hot and thick. It slid along her skin, and she swore her cunt clenched in an effort to pull the liquid into her, to complete her.

But she remained unfulfilled. It was a physical ache.

Tucking himself away, he examined her, pausing to watch his cum drip along her slit. His chest puffed out, proud, satisfied. Flicking his gaze back up to hers, he ordered, "If you move one inch, we do this all over again."

Again? The thought invigorated her tears. It wasn't over *now*. Her body was still shaking and screaming for release.

But she swallowed and nodded.

"Good girl."

· · · · ● · ● · · ·

Rogan left her on the table for what seemed like hours but in reality was probably less than one. To distract herself from her throbbing pussy—she swore she was so wet she leaked onto the table—she concentrated on how her skin itched from his dried cum and the salt water. It was less irritating than the gold paint had been.

The torment was of her own creation. She had little to occupy her mind, so she fantasized about how he would let her come. Would he suck her clit? Fuck her hard and fast? Or slow, sliding his hard length languorously in and out of her? Her imaginings increased her need.

After a torturous dinner, which she was allowed to prepare, he tied her spread eagle to the bed. It jogged the strangest memory. Why now, when he'd tied her before, she didn't understand. But clear as day, the mental images slammed into her brain. Ones of being held down, naked, on a hospital bed when she had been about three.

The experience was one she had forgotten. But the second the images appeared, it felt like yesterday. She was screaming, sobbing, viciously fighting against the people who struggled to restrain her. She didn't want to be spread out for them. It was wrong. She knew it. She'd felt a sense of pride that even as four adults attempted to keep her still, she continued to kick and hit and shriek without pause.

Along with the fear, the rage, and the wrongness she'd felt, she remembered a sense of embarrassment, as well.

How would she know, at the age of three, that being naked and on display wasn't right? That it wasn't normal? That it was a violation?

21

NARLINA

Rogan

Rogan tucked a strand of hair behind her ear as he studied her profile. Her eyes flashed over to him, gauged quickly that his action was that simple, and then she returned her attention to adding ingredients into their noontime omelets.

The tension was sky high. It had been charged since yesterday. Every one of her movements screamed for relief; she was jumpy from overstimulation, not fear. She was probably praying for the moment he allowed her to come. Her obedience and restraint impressed him. She could have gotten off at any time, really, but she hadn't.

Or maybe she couldn't have. He had tied her to the bed, spread eagle, in order to keep her from seeking release in her sleep. He'd taken advantage of the open field of her body, teasing her even more by sucking and palming her tits. She'd twisted and panted, straining against her bonds. She was glorious, with her flushed cheeks and pleading eyes.

"Do you like this punishment?" he asked.

She ducked her head as though she could hide her conflict from him or didn't know how she should respond. She peeked at him as though she was searching for a clue to the correct answer. He'd stroked the edges of her pussy lips, causing her to thrash, to seek his hand where she needed it. "The truth, little prize. I'll know if you're lying."

Her blush had deepened. After three breaths, she gave him a hesitant, tiny nod. He'd smiled and collared her neck beneath the leather. Her pulse raced under his hand. It thrilled him that she liked this torment. It wasn't only about the sex. It was about the trust she must have for him to want this.

Yes, gratifying him was implicit in her role, but her submission was hers to give. She could hate everything he and Wes did to her, and she probably had initially, but not now. Her arousal, her acceptance of her punishment, and her faith in him to know when the time was right, excited and humbled him. Staring at her swollen, glistening pussy, he'd been tempted to slip inside her.

"It's a punishment for me, too." He'd nuzzled the pulsing vein in her neck. "All I want to do is fuck you, but I deserve just a taste of this torture for taking my eyes off you." It was true. His dick was painfully hard, but he would wait. "If you're a good girl, your reward will be fucking mind-blowing."

She moved away from him with the bowl of seasoned eggs, stirring still, and turned her concentration to the hot pan. Propped up against the counter, Rogan folded his arms over his chest and watched her. Her culinary skills were top-notch, as far as he could tell. On the rare occasion he'd given her free rein of the kitchen, she had been creative with flavors. Her mastery now in flipping the omelet in the pan was impressive.

Was cooking a hobby, a profession?

Over and over, he told himself he didn't want to know. It was a dangerous path to take, imagining her life on the mainland. It would tease his need to be there and throw it in her face that she no longer was, nor would she be returning. Like her voice, it was a part of her past. There was no way he could hear about it without blaming her.

Uncomfortably, he acknowledged that he didn't want to know about her life before because it meant there was a place for her to return to, an opportunity for her to leave him. Betray him. It was fucked up to worry about his possession slipping through his fingers. After yesterday, though…

He pushed away from the counter and moved to the kitchen table. She was distracting. For a silent woman, her presence was loud. He'd never been more aware of a person than he was of her. Not even Narlina captivated him like his pet did.

· · · • · • • · · ·

"Narlina is in the park. She's waiting for us," Wes announced as he stepped inside the apartment. His tone was one of disinterest, his attention divided between the topic and the woman in the corner.

Rogan's pulse leaped. His brain responded with a dose of giddy adrenaline before he put the reaction in a stranglehold. The look she'd tossed him at the beach wasn't one to inspire excitement on his part. Then again, he was tense with unreleased energy. "Alone?" He didn't want to deal with Alan right now, especially after the foreboding sense he'd gotten yesterday.

Wes smirked. "As alone as a park can be. But it's something." He studied his doll more thoroughly, his brow furrowing as though he could scent her arousal, as though he could tell she was suffering. But he cleared his throat and turned his full attention on Rogan. "We need to go now."

Rogan snapped, "Prize, let's go."

"Just us, man." Wes rubbed the back of his neck, frowning in disappointment. "She has to stay."

Rogan's reaction was just as distressed, though the feeling was mixed with puzzlement over his instinct to bring her along.

Quickly, he pushed away the sentiment, dismissing it as a reaction to her pathetic escape attempt.

She was still firmly in the grips of the consequences of her actions. Her continued agitated expression told him she was still hovering in her state of arousal. Her frequent shifting on her bed signaled that despite the foam, her ass was still raw. He didn't want that wasted because he had to step away.

He resigned himself to shackling her to the bedpost. She'd probably get herself off the moment they left, but he couldn't concern himself with that at the moment. Narlina was waiting.

Wes looked pissed that Rogan had restrained her, but really, it was for her safety. It would save her from herself, from attempting to flee again. Or worse, attempting to take herself out of his reach in another manner.

After securing her, they left the apartment. He strode beside Wes along flagstones, telling himself that the lingering need to have his pet accompany him was because he wanted to taunt Narlina with her presence. He wanted to fawn and pet his prize, show Narlina their marks on her flesh. He'd noted the hurt in her expression the other day, and he wanted to wring more of those looks out of her.

Also, he'd taken Ruff almost everywhere with him, so why wouldn't he treat this pet in the same manner? The water might have been a disaster, but the park would be a safe place where she would have little possibility of getting herself into trouble. Ruff had loved the park, not that he expected his prize would frolic freely if he brought her here. He couldn't imagine her running around in glee when he unhooked her leash. Running, he could see, but not frolicking. Her silent presence was also becoming habitual. Comfortable.

Of course, he had taken a shine to fucking her, too. He loved it almost as much as he loved to watch her squirm with need.

His focus should be on Narlina. He concentrated on keeping his steps languid rather than running. Despite Wes's chatter, his thoughts wandered to his pet back home. He wouldn't dissect the reasons why.

They approached the tree-lined space with its ostentatious fountain in the middle. It was a cheap replica of the fountain in Savannah, Georgia; he'd taken a tech class there once. He'd enjoyed the city's culture and atmosphere, the vibe. The island's version of the fountain was scaled down, of course, and gaudily out of place in the tiny park.

But all thoughts about the fountain's origin and his prize left him when he saw her. Even Wes's monologue was shut out. He was deaf and blind to everything and everyone except her.

Narlina.

She stood in profile, the waters cascading behind her. Her red hair fell down the length of her back; she was a siren—his siren—and true to her nature as such, she had him on the point of death. Her blue dress was a shimmering silk sheath perfectly molded to every curve. He'd touched and kissed and worshipped those curves, worshipped her.

"Blink. Breathe." Wes's order permeated. "I guess I don't need to worry about you murdering her in broad daylight if your dick is hard and your brain is on stun."

Rogan frowned. "Neither one of those is true."

"So, I *do* need to worry that you'll try to drown her in the fountain?"

"Wes." The word was a rebuke and a warning. However, he was silently cursing the surge of regretful love that almost overpowered him.

To his credit, his pace didn't falter; he didn't stumble over his own feet at the sight of her. He maintained his stride and his stoic expression when she turned her head and caught sight of him. A bolt of fear flashed across her face as she spied him. In response, he was simultaneously satisfied and stung by the need to soothe her distress. Worrying her lip, she dragged her attention over to Wes. A moment later, when she turned those ice-blue eyes back on him, she had composed herself, her expression neutral and her chin held high.

As he and Wes reached the concrete circling the fountain, she clasped her hands in front of her, affecting a serene disposition. But the tightness with which she clenched her fingers betrayed her.

"Rogan. Wes."

Her voice, which had once soothed him, now enraged him. How could she stand there so calmly, regard him with cool detachment, when they'd meant the world to each other only weeks ago? This moment was more surreal than the first time he'd stepped onto the mainland, when the crowded busyness of it had been daunting. Back before his soul leaped into the madness and became addicted.

"Narlina."

"Thank you both for coming." Her voice was shaky.

The tremor was subtle, but it intensified his satisfaction. After what she'd done, she should be terrified to face him without her husband present. Then again, he admired her courage, even if it had taken this long for her to muster it. Maybe their run-in yesterday had bolstered her. Narlina was a gentle woman. She was purposefully blind to the atrocities her husband committed and allowed to occur; her tender heart couldn't handle it. She knew. Of course she did. But for her own mental health, she chose not to see.

"I have so much I want to say to you."

Rogan frowned. Her tone was monotone, the words stiff, like she was reading from a script. He wanted to look at Wes, to gauge his reaction to this automaton in front of them. Instead, he responded warily. "I'm eager for whatever you have to say." His stare was intent, pointed, and silently demanded answers.

She shuffled in place, her hands twisting so severely her knuckles were white.

As she hesitated, he studied her face, looking for further distress. Her masks rarely fooled him. Today was no different. She looked like she wanted to crumple in the face of his frank assessment. Maybe beg him for forgiveness. At one time, it would have been her natural response.

And he needed it: open contrition. He needed her tears. Yet all he received was a wavering façade. Knowing she had to protect herself from him in this way was gratifying. He narrowed his eyes slightly, hoping the move conveyed clearly that he didn't forgive her. That he saw through her and found her pathetic.

Children; they'd known and loved each other since childhood, and she dared to stand before him as a stranger now. She had to know he was barely hanging on to his temper. Then, maybe not. With her, he'd never been the angry man he was now, the one she'd created in a second.

"Are you going to send smoke signals or tell us?" Wes's tone was light, yet it was laced with distrust and uncertainty, and as he asked, he scanned the area, the people. They knew almost everyone on the island—except the pampered, sheltered guests. Wes was tense, looking for a threat.

Rogan was slow to put the pieces together, but they finally clicked. Wes didn't need to be here for this conversation, yet they had both been summoned. This place was surrounded by surveillance cameras. He was no threat to her here.

That, and the nervousness and stalling, led him to believe she was a decoy. But why?

He had been so eager to see her, to get his answers from her, that he hadn't stopped to consider anything other than what had been presented: Narlina wanted to talk to him. Because Wes had been their cover before, it seemed normal.

Rogan lifted his hand and motioned with two fingers. The move caused a flash of his prize's pussy to cross his mind. Forcing the image away, he prompted, "Start talking."

Narlina tilted her chin higher. She was going for imperious. The attempt was wasted on him. "Ro," she appealed. She glanced at Wes and her brows drew together briefly. Was she noticing his suspicious watchfulness?

"Tell me why." It was all he wanted to know, so he might as well get to the heart of it straight away. Although, in this case, there was no *heart*.

She focused on him again. Her beautiful blue eyes begged him; for what, he wasn't sure. The look of apology turned his stomach; he'd seen it before. That day. But there was no reason for her to give it again, surely. In his periphery, Wes turned to look behind them.

"I was scared. You can't blame me for being scared. You can't stop loving me for being scared." She looked down demurely, lashes fluttering. "You still love me, don't you?"

Yes. No. Fuck her.

"You could have told me," he ground out. "You know you could have told me. Instead, you laid out your deceit for all to witness. Do you know how fucking hard it was to stay on my feet when you tore my heart out in front of them?"

"You do love me," she said in relief.

"My devotion for you runs as deep as yours for me."

Her face brightened for a second, then dropped when his meaning sank in. *Dropped* because she wasn't devoted to him. His words called her out. They both knew it.

"Did you tell anyone?" He was pretty sure she hadn't, or he'd be a dead man now; not that he wasn't allowed to buy his way off the island, but because he'd planned on taking her, too.

Her irritated expression comforted him. "Of course not."

"Are we done here?" Wes asked. He was increasingly edgy, shifting on his feet.

"Not yet," she murmured.

She continued to speak in an apologetic tone, her expression beseeching.

Rogan's heart thudded, sensing the danger Wes was trying to locate. "Out with it."

"When... I mean. It wasn't supposed to happen the way it did. You were given the wrong prize." She tossed an accusing look toward Wes. "Allow me to give you something else. Anything else."

The jolt nearly knocked him off his feet. For one second, hope surged forward. A hope that she would tell him he'd be given the money after all. But it was dashed in the next instant. Prizes weren't revocable; mistakes didn't happen.

Clearly sensing the same dread, Wes turned around completely, staring in the direction from whence they'd come.

"Prizes are irrevocable," Rogan pointed out. "If a mistake was made, I would be allowed to take a new one and keep the original." He couldn't help his smirk as he said it. "Because I'm keeping her."

Her nostrils flared, and her face went pink. She'd received his message and she didn't like it. With her chin tilted, she gave him a cold scowl. "You're not."

"What do you mean?" Wes asked before Rogan could, shifting so he could both watch their backs and ask her directly.

"Your errant prize is being recycled. We'll find—"

Rogan didn't hear the rest. He was already in motion.

22

KITTY, KITTY
The Prize

Rogan had cuffed her to the bedpost for the first time since she'd started sharing the bed with them. At least he'd dragged in the dog bed for her. Early on, it had been routine to drag it behind her when she was shuffled from one room to the next, but it had remained in the front room since they'd started fucking.

If she could talk, she would point out that she would behave. Not that he would believe her after yesterday. And she had no desire to kill him. She'd heard more than once that cutting the head off a snake left room for two to grow back. She already sort of had two: her owner and Wes. She didn't want four in their stead.

Her former lover—she didn't know what he was now; it certainly wasn't love—had watched with a speculative expression as Rogan had shackled her. His gaze had prowled hungrily over her. Neither of them hid their desire for her. It was heady, assisting her in the delusion that lust equaled emotions. There'd been a curl to his upper lip that looked like distaste or disagreement. Not for her, but because Rogan was securing the other cuff.

Wes might like the aesthetic of her collar, and he liked tying her up during sex—she liked it, too—but from the look on his face before they'd left, he didn't support staking her to the bedpost like she was a goat. There was a hint of the man she'd known in the disapproving microexpression.

What the hell had he thought would happen to her once he'd brought her here? He'd taken her and allowed her to be raped so many times she lost count. But he was bothered by a pair of leather-wrapped cuffs—that he'd provided—that bound her to a solid-wood post?

Laying her head on her arm, she stared sightlessly at the wall, pushing the consistent throb of her clit from her mind. This was her punishment. She deserved it. Deep in her soul, she liked it, too. She hadn't lied. The build-up, excruciating as it was, would be worth it. When Rogan allowed her to come, she'd transform for that space of time. Maybe the longer she was denied, the farther the catapult.

Because there was no other option, she concentrated on the pattern of the drywall and the faint strokes from the paint roller. Boredom would eventually eat at her brain. She would become catatonic with the lack of stimulation. Cooking occasional meals helped, but it wasn't enough to keep her mind occupied beyond the extent of the task. If she could work up the bravery, she could sneak one of Rogan's books off his shelf. Her heart and soul ached for words on a page to transport her.

But how would she hide it from him? Under the dog bed? Or in it?

For the first time since her captivity, she was excited about something beyond how their bodies made hers feel. Sitting up, she investigated the seams for a zipper. She was only able to turn the bed beneath her, considering her range wasn't great. She was hopeful. It seemed as though most dog beds had removable covers so they could be cleaned.

Her fingers had just discovered the metallic track, sending a wave of elation through her, when the front door opened. She froze, listening intently; they hadn't been gone long, though it had been long enough to give her hope that she could sneak a book.

Over the pounding of her heart, though, she heard them.

"Where is she?"

"Fuck if I know. They didn't take her with them. They were told not to."

Instantly, she was yanked back into the hell of her first weeks, the terror she was still emerging from. Those voices didn't belong to her men.

The heavy footsteps spurred her to action. She scooted under the bed, her heart lurching when her ass didn't want to go, almost causing her to sob out loud. Despite the pain, she shoved herself under the wooden frame. She'd have scrapes and bruises. Her ass, still smarting from the spanking, burned and throbbed from the additional treatment. But she made it under.

Her bed had been kicked askew, but there was no time to straighten it, if she could even reach it. She slid back as far from the edge as she could, pulling the chain with her slowly so it wouldn't make a sound. To that end, she buried her face in her arm to muffle the sounds of her panicked breaths.

As they approached, she silently begged for her men to appear, for Rogan to miraculously return and save her, to aggressively shove these people away, as he had on their walk to the clinic. But for them to move about so boldly, slamming open doors and possibly cabinets and leisurely stroll down the hall to her, took confidence. They were certain they wouldn't be interrupted. Her men wouldn't save her.

"Here, kitty, kitty." The familiar sarcastic drawl made her stomach roll and had her holding her breath so she wouldn't burst into tears.

She didn't want to go back there, back to the room where she'd last heard that voice, with the cages and cold and lessons, to the torturous positions and manipulations she hadn't known a body could be forced into, used for. That which she had survived as a child hadn't been in the same realm; the perpetrators of her youth had no imagination.

There was no limit to the imagination of *these* perpetrators, and she hadn't been in that facility for the allotted amount of time. Wes had pulled her out for Rogan. Were they back to finish her twisted education? Had her men been too cowardly to stand here and watch her be taken away? To admit they'd tired of her? Was this because of yesterday? She was their willing and submissive toy, their doll to take pleasure from. She didn't want to go back to that hellhole.

No, no, no.

"There you are, little kitty."

She had been lost in her world of memory and fear. Then suddenly, peering at her, was a familiar face. The face of a man who'd sneered as he'd shoved his dick in her mouth, the mouth that had been forced open. She consumed and gagged on more of his disgusting-tasting cum in a few weeks than she had enjoyed ice cream her entire life.

"Under the bed. It's where all kitties go to hide." He reached out, swiping his arm along the floor, and she jerked away. "Fighting makes it worse. You know that."

How would she know that, other than from what she'd witnessed? She'd never fought back. But she would now. If her rebellion ended her, then she would embrace that eventuality. She would *not* go back to the existence she'd been forced into before falling at Rogan's feet.

Scooting and wriggling away from him, she kept her attention fixed on the enemy she could see. So she almost pissed herself with dread and fear when her leg was grasped.

The other voice crowed in triumph. "Got her!"

No, no, no.

She kicked and flailed as much as her confines would allow. His grip slipped once or twice, but it was no use. She didn't have the speed or the space to completely escape, and eventually, the two of them dragged her out from under the bed. Her ass took another scraping and bruising, but the pain was almost imperceptible. Her stunned body was going numb.

From the moment she was brought struggling, squirming, and kicking from her hiding spot, she was all motion and fight. She kicked viciously at the man who grabbed her foot and dragged her away from the bed. She wore nothing more than one of Rogan's shirts, and it had ridden up in her struggles so they saw her pussy and her ass, but in this moment, the modicum of modesty she was allowed didn't matter.

Her shoulders and wrists were suddenly set on fire as she was tugged so forcefully she was sure one of her body parts would fail her and dislocate. Her stupid captors hadn't realized she was trapped until they'd almost torn her apart.

"What the fuck?"

Despite the shrieking burn in her arms, she maintained her silence. Gasps, grunts, and whimpers accompanied her thrashing legs and wiggling body, but she remained silent. Rogan hadn't given her leave to use her voice.

She was unceremoniously dropped, though the man clung tight to her leg. Feet stomped near her head, and she cringed away. Her wrist was shaken, shooting more shards of pain up her arm.

"Unbuckle the cuffs." The voice of the enemy behind her was full of irritation.

She renewed her bucking and kicked out with her free leg. She focused all she had on landing a good blow, maybe to his jaw, or better yet, she should aim for his mushroom-shaped dick that tasted like the fungus it represented.

Instead, her flailing ankle was captured. He jerked her back, sending a white-hot pain coursing through her. She opened her mouth in a silent shriek, then sucked in a sharp breath.

"Needs a fucking key," the one next to her snarled.

Pain ricocheted through her, this time from the punch that was delivered to the back of her head. Stars danced in front of her eyes.

"Fucking bitch."

She groaned, giving up her fight, and rested her cheek against the floor.

"Lift the bed."

"It's solid wood. Faster to cut her hand off."

She whimpered in response. She wouldn't put it past them. Her body trembled. Her mind betrayed her, instantly creating images of a life without her hand. She needed her hands. Her profession... She'd need her hands to—

"Goddamn weak son of a bitch."

Her legs were released. Unexpectedly free, they hit the floor before she could control the drop.

Her rapist crowded them at the post. "When I push up, get the chain out from under." He braced himself beneath the footboard, his booted feet planted wide.

It took him three tries. During the second attempt, the post fell on the chain, smashing it, but by the third, she slipped free. Only, not free. Because they had her. Her earlier fear paled in comparison to the perils she now faced.

They had her.

She was hauled to her feet, but if they thought she would walk out of here with them, they were mistaken. Despite her throbbing head, the numbness in her arms, and her minuscule odds of escaping them, she fought. In her mind's eye, she was a feral cat: spitting, biting, flailing. She braced her bare feet against the floor, refusing to budge. It was for naught.

"Move, you useless whore!"

She did the opposite. She dropped down, dead weight, wanting to be as difficult as possible. However, she underestimated their disregard for her and her pain. She shouldn't have. Not after the nightmare they'd put her through already. In response to her action, she was kicked once more. Then one of the men grasped the collar around her neck and dragged her from the room.

Choking, she kicked and flailed even harder than before, her fingers digging at the leather biting into her neck.

Her terror grew. No air, no mercy, no escaping her fate.

But this was fine, her mind screamed. Dying here would be better than surviving only to end up back in the cages. The dancing lights, the muffled voices and yells, the tile tearing at her skin as she was dragged along, was fine. She hadn't been made for this life anyway; how many times did that fact need to be reinforced before she gave in? Death would be salvation.

23

PUNISHMENT

Rogan

Theft wasn't tolerated here. Crime was addressed quickly and severely in order to control the island's occupants. Punishment was dealt out swiftly and harshly. In this instance, Rogan and Wes hadn't waited for the island's justice; they doled it out themselves.

The dead man had touched his possession. He'd dared to attempt to drag his prize out of Rogan's apartment. The other man would be in the clinic for a while before being turned over to a fate worse than jail.

Was Rogan worried about the repercussions for killing a man? No.

The second Narlina uttered that word—recycled—he'd understood. And he'd run, with Wes on his heels. Neither gave pause to Narlina as she screamed after him that it was too late. Fuck that; it wasn't too late until he saw with his own eyes that his prize was no longer in his possession.

The taking Narlina had apparently arranged—she had to have, based on this encounter—was outside the boundaries of the island's strictly enforced laws. If gifts were taken away, then people would become angry, suspicious—more so than some already were—and make demands.

Alan needed them happy, docile, so he could manage the island and the nefarious secrets it kept. Therefore, whoever was repossessing—trying to repossess—that which had been given to him did not have the authority to do so.

He pushed himself faster, desperate to get to his apartment before she was removed from it. If he didn't make it, a case could be made, cuffs or not, that she'd tried to run.

As he burst through his open doorway, his heart stuttered. They had been so close to taking her, just steps from dragging her limp body out. He didn't stop to consider the scene or ask questions; he launched.

The two perpetrators were in the wrong, but they'd fought back as though they were on the side of right. Maybe Narlina had convinced them it was so. Regardless, his brutal and battering fists pointed out the error of their ways. Wes jumped in with him without hesitation. Rogan's fist had met his opponent's face one second after that man had called out Wes's name.

Whether they knew one another or not was inconsequential to Rogan. Considering the fury with which Wes followed him into the short-lived fray, the acquaintance wasn't important. It was over quickly. Rogan wasn't interested in humoring these fuckers; he dispatched the man by shoving his nose into his brain.

The man dropped to the ground beside his bruised, bloody, and unconscious prize. Whether he'd killed her or not, the thief deserved to pay with his life. Though if she was dead, he would be pissed that he hadn't drawn the thief's own death out. Before he could pay her much attention, he helped Wes. The moment the second thief was knocked out, Wes was on his knees next to her.

Shaking out his fist and moving his jaw back and forth to ensure it was still in place, Rogan watched his friend gingerly pick up the woman and cradle her to his chest.

"Hey, Doll. Baby doll." Wes wiped her dark hair from her bruising face.

Rogan strove for dispassion as Wes performed a perfunctory and uninformed exam. She was breathing, but she'd been through what looked like a fight of her own. Her neck was red and beginning to both bruise and swell around her collar. The bleeding scratches and tile burn told their own story.

Wes cursed as he moved his hand through her hair. "Fuckers hit her head. She has a knot."

"She could have hit her own head," Rogan pointed out. It wasn't to give the assholes an out, but it looked like she'd battled hard not to be taken. Secretly, he liked it, knowing she'd gone down—presumably—fighting. It meant she was fighting to remain his.

Wes shook his head, his expression grim. He looked over at the one living man, and that look morphed into one of contemplative rage, as if he was considering finishing him off. The reaction was far too intense to be concern over his friend's prize almost being stolen.

But of course it was. Because Wes had wanted her for himself; the depth of the man's devotion to her—despite everything—was evident. The unexpected surge of jealousy that rose up in Rogan was foreign and bewildering.

A scream drew his attention to the open door. Narlina stood at the threshold, hands to her mouth, and surveyed the scene with frightened eyes. Then she homed in on the woman cradled in Wes's arms. A flash of relief washed over her. Was it because Wes was the one with his arms around the woman, or because he and Wes were still alive?

"These men—are they dead?" she asked, dropping her hands from her face.

Rogan didn't answer her. Her concern wasn't for the men she considered dispensable—after all, that's why she'd sent them. She knew they would be punished, even if they'd been successful.

Her devastating blue eyes swung to him, surveyed him—the blood—and he swore she swayed toward him, her instincts as on point as Wes's to take care of what was hers. No, not hers. He never had been.

"You ran from me." Her tone was laced with hurt, betrayal. Good.

"I ran to protect what is mine," he said quietly, evenly.

God, the look of torment that crossed her features forced him to fight his own instincts to go to her, to reassure her. If she'd come to him with tears of remorse rather than with a duplicitous scheme to take more from him, he very well may have crumpled at her feet. He almost had, as it was. Wes's uncanny suspicion was all that had kept him from caving. If she'd sweetly asked it of him, he might have willingly given over the prize just to have her back in his arms.

But now? Fuck that. Fuck her. She had been fueled by jealousy, selfishness, and narcissism today. Not love. So he didn't owe her that in return.

Her scream brought others to the doorway.

"Is that man dead?"

"That's Brad."

"What's going on?"

Rogan shrugged, striving to appear unruffled. He glanced at the dead man and his unfortunately living accomplice, then addressed his neighbors. "They tried to steal from me."

He looked back at the gawkers, at Narlina. Her already alabaster complexion whitened even more. She looked at him with something he'd never seen before—fear.

Yes, fear me, you lying, traitorous bitch. He didn't say it, but his message was received. Her eyes widened.

"Get someone to clear them out of here," he commanded.

A man in the doorway answered in the affirmative before stepping away. Another curious onlooker took his place.

"Brad was a trainer. What is he doing up here?"

"He's not a trainer anymore. He's now a thief and a dead man," Wes said from the floor.

Rogan didn't turn to look at him; his enemy was in the doorway, and her ways were much more stealthy. He didn't trust her enough to turn his gaze from her for long.

Narlina looked behind him, her expression annoyed. "You worked with him. He trained that *slave*." The last word was spit out with distaste.

Rogan was doubly glad the man was dead, then, if he was a trainer. One who'd touched his pet, others.

Narlina regarded Rogan again. Far too late, she conjured those tears that had motivated him before today to drop to his knees and promise her anything. *Just please don't be sad; don't cry*. Now, he wanted her tears. He wanted her sadness.

It wasn't loyalty to the probably dead woman behind him. He didn't owe her loyalty. It was recognizing that the one in front of him didn't love him; it was because of her lack of loyalty, of faith. "You need to go—all of you."

"Rogan," she whispered, shaking her head. "You don't understand."

"Go. I need to tend to her." He added with flair, for those observing the scene, "Your generous nature gave her to me. Because of that, I will cherish her always." The words escaped through clenched teeth. He despised Narlina and the woman behind him equally, but he would defend what he owned.

Tears spilled down Narlina's cheeks, but there was another emotion there, too: hatred.

They were on common ground once again.

24

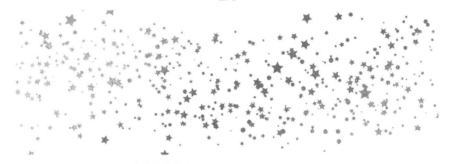

ATTACHMENT
The Prize

Awareness was a tricky thing. She transitioned from the comforting dark to being aware of sound. Quickly, her brain raced to interpret the stimulus. Before she opened her eyes, she knew two things: one, she hadn't died; and two, Wes was talking to her, urging her to wake up.

She didn't want to open her eyes, to acknowledge that she was still drifting in her hellish reality. She wanted to keep her eyes closed and slip back into the darkness, never to emerge. She'd been so close.

Pain ricocheted through her. Her neck, her head, her body. The cool air that brushed her pussy warned her that she was exposed. Her nudity no longer mattered.

"C'mon, Doll."

A jostle accompanied his words. It hurt; she moaned. Tears slid out from beneath her eyelids.

"There you are. Come on back to me."

No, she didn't want to. But the choice, as with so many things, wasn't hers. Just as her eyelashes fluttered, Rogan roughly grasped her upper arm and ripped her away from Wes. Then he was dragging her out the door, adding to the scrapes and bruises that littered her body. Pain exploded in her head from the sudden movement; her entire body rebelled.

Outside, a small crowd had gathered. Their expressions ranged from curious to defensive. The beautiful woman from yesterday was standing there, eyes wide and mouth agape. The expression was mostly one of shock, but there was an underlying anger there, too, when their eyes met.

Her attention was snatched away from the glaring blue-eyed woman when Rogan stopped and dropped her to the ground. Her heart thudded with dread. Why was he throwing her away? She knew to expect it, but why? Why now?

"This is my reward, *my* prize. *I* earned her."

Some responses were those of agreement, others were confused; a few accused. One voice shouted about a dead man; others pointed out that she was only a sex slave. Head aching, she turned her gaze upward and focused on Rogan as she tried to make sense of the words tossed in the air around them—a dead man? That hadn't been her doing. Above her, Rogan unbuttoned and unzipped his jeans, then pulled out his dick. There were no gasps or outcries of indecency. Oddly, she'd expected them, even though she knew all too well what this place—this island—was meant for.

"Maybe this is something you'll understand."

She dropped her head, her trembling increasing. He was going to fuck her publicly. And they would all watch; had probably been hoping for a moment like this since she'd landed at his feet. His careless disregard of her hurt when it shouldn't have. She was a tool, a dumb body that he would use until he tired of her and moved on to the next.

When hot liquid hit her head in a forceful stream, raining over her, she startled. Stunned, she raised her hands and watched his urine drip off her. *He was peeing on her.* Instead of horrification, a surge of understanding overtook her, and another emotion, a powerful one she couldn't name, emerged with it. She found solace in the moment. Because he was marking her. *Claiming* her.

Gasps and exclamations surrounded them now. As well as a few chuckles and several moans of appreciation. Wes's voice rang out as he laughingly admonished Rogan for pissing on her when she had open wounds on her neck. But she felt no pain.

From under the stream, she peered up at him, and their eyes locked. He blinked rapidly, as though taken aback by the visual connection. But he didn't falter. When he finished, he loosely tucked himself away. As he did so, her attention was drawn to the movement, and her heart leaped at the sight of his partially swollen cock. Pissing on her turned him on.

With a grunt, he yanked her to her feet, and rather than forcing her to attempt to stand on her own, he bent and threw her over his shoulder. Without another word, he spun, and with her dripping his piss all over him and the ground, he returned to the apartment.

He set her in the shower and grasped her face. His dark eyes were earnest. "If anyone other than me or Wes touches you, you scream." His hands shook against her skin; whether it was left over adrenaline or not, she wanted to interpret it as fear. Fear that he'd almost lost her. "You're mine. Do you understand me?"

She nodded, blinking at him through her tears and the quickly cooling liquid dripping from her.

His. She was his, demonstratively so. Her silly heart thudded with hope.

25

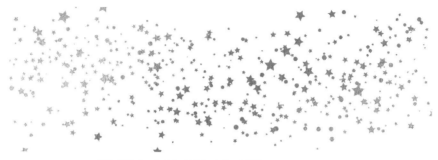

CONSEQUENCES

Rogan

He'd never pissed on anyone; hadn't known it was in him to do so. His prize was teaching him many things about himself. But he'd been enraged by the audacity of anyone—*Narlina* especially—who would try to take something that had been given to him; what was his.

Narlina had looked on in horror at his actions, her lips parted and her face drained of all color, as she stood at the crowd's edge, acting as though she hadn't been the orchestrator of the scene playing out. But his pet, the woman curled into a ball on the ground below him, wasn't repulsed. Her expression had been one of appreciation and gratitude.

He'd gotten off on it, that look, her obedient acceptance of what others might interpret as degradation, disgusting. That wasn't why he'd done it, and, innately, she knew it.

Still reeking of his piss despite the water crashing down on them from the showerhead, he pulled her to him. He kissed her, taking what he'd not taken before, her mouth. His tongue slipped in, demanding. Her fervor met his own, stoking his need higher. They were both desperate, hands roving and tugging at clothing, filled with the need to press flesh against flesh. She was already tightly wound, ready to give him her all.

This was a claiming. Or at least, another one.

They were behaving like equals. In a sense, they were, both being owned—but their desire for gratification overrode the reality of their roles. He pulled the shirt over her head and tossed it outside the tub. Clinging to her nape with one hand, he used the other to push his wet jeans and shorts down only far enough to free his hard cock. She winced as he gripped her, but she didn't slow. He didn't either. Her hands were on his chest, and she scraped her nails across his flesh, causing him to hiss into her mouth; it was erotic, this woman's nails scoring him.

He lifted her, and her legs automatically wrapped around his waist. Her arms, too, knew what to do, winding around his neck. She clung to him. With one arm lashed around her back, he turned and pressed her against the tiles. He steadied himself, then buried himself deep inside her. Fast, furious, panting. She made a noise in her throat, which had to be sore, and buried her face in his neck as he pounded into her.

"This pussy, this tight pussy, is mine. You'll give it to me whenever I want it. I've earned you through what you've stolen from me." He sped up.

She wriggled in his arms, her legs tightening around him as she bucked against him.

"I'll take what's owed me from your pretty cunt."

That was all it took for her to disintegrate. Her body shook in his arms. She opened her mouth to suck in air, and when she exhaled, her breath hit his flesh, and tiny sounds escaped her. He fucking loved the control she had over her voice when she was coming hard; loved it because he'd ordered it, and she obeyed.

He fucked her through her orgasm. His balls tightened further when he realized he pleasured her so thoroughly that she was lost in one long, continuous release. Resolutely, he left it there. He loved being the master of her body. Nothing more. But less than an hour after nearly being killed, after being strangled and beaten so badly her body was covered in scrapes and bruises, *and* after he'd pissed on her, she was coming around his cock. She was holding on to him like he was her salvation.

In a sense, he was.

When he came, he gave a voice to them both.

Drained and exhausted, he fell against her, pressing her into the tiles. Her arms and legs tightened around him as she snuggled closer. Her hair still smelled like urine, his urine. They hadn't bathed, just fucked.

Reluctantly, he pulled back. Taking her cue as he slipped from her, she stood on her own. Her cheeks were bright red. Though one might think it was from her injuries, he was certain it was a blush. After everything she'd been through, she was blushing. Fuck, she was a puzzle, and her capacity to surprise him was fathomless.

He gave her a quick kiss at the temple. "No more cuffing you when I'm gone. You're free to roam, pet."

• • • • • • • • •

If he thought his actions wouldn't have consequences, he was fooling himself. Not from the killing, but from his demonstration. His defense of her had been extreme. It showed a deeper connection than was expected of a person and their slaves. Infatuation was one thing; desire was understood. But to blur lines with feelings, to show empathy—although one could argue his actions were not compassionate—was a red flag. It threatened to tip the balance, create chaos in a tightly controlled environment.

After their shower, where he took pride and pleasure in making her clean, despite his misgivings—not for his actions, but for the repercussions—he tucked her into his bed. Wes had been waiting for them with an ointment and carefully applied it to her neck.

Despite his assurances, he cuffed one of her wrists to the headboard; it was more about how it looked than trust. Besides, he was here.

She hadn't given him a side-eye or an expression of disappointment. Wes had, but not her. They both kissed her good night—Wes dallying so long that Rogan dragged him back—before leaving her to sleep. She needed to sleep; it was the fastest way for a body to heal. He didn't look the truth in the face, that he *was* beginning to look at her the way Wes did. Instead, he told himself that he needed to take care of his things; that's all it was: possessiveness, not attachment, even though the panic he'd experienced yesterday was nothing compared to the fear that had gripped him as he'd raced back today.

Once they'd retreated to the kitchen, he withdrew two beers from the refrigerator.

The injured and dead men were gone. He and Wes exchanged grave expressions. "Thank you, man."

Wes shook his head, his lip curled in disgust. "Thank fuck I was there. My doll would be dead, and you'd be a groveling fool sniffing around that bitch."

Rage pumped through him at Wes's words. They hit too close to the truth. Though rather than admitting it, he threw another truth out, "You killed her the moment you brought her here."

Wes took a startled step back, eyes widening. In the next second, his expression turned thunderous. That look spoke for itself; the reluctant acknowledgment, the fury at being called out. His own fear.

"You know slaves don't have longevity here. Why do this to her if you care about her?"

His friend tilted his head and furrowed his brow in curious challenge. "Since when do you care?"

Rogan turned away. That wasn't his question or his point. He deflected, as Wes just had. "She's a target. Alan's taken notice. Narlina wants her dead. Do you think this will be the only attempt? She wants me stuck here, *for her*, and without another woman."

He grimaced.

"I'm *her* pet, her prize, and she wants to control me."

Wes let out a breath and nodded.

Rogan glanced toward the hallway and made sure to speak clearly, loudly, to justify it to himself more than anything. "My authority in the community won't be undermined by allowing others to take what's mine."

Wes's expression was skeptical when Rogan turned back, as if he were surprised by that reasoning. "I can't go anywhere without her."

"They won't let you take her to the communications room."

Rogan rubbed the back of his neck, a knot twisting in his gut. "Would you take shifts with me?"

Wes looked at him with mirth. It *was* comical, arranging for his sex slave to have a babysitter.

"I brought her here for me; we've had this discussion. No, I don't have a problem having more access to her."

So that was the reason for his expression. "Then help me keep her safe while I figure this shit out."

"What shit?"

Rogan glanced around his apartment before he looked at Wes again, pointedly. "Shit."

Wes nodded, though a little apprehensively, as understanding dawned. "Okay, buddy. You need to do you."

Rogan didn't bother correcting Wes's assumption that only he would be leaving the island. Because when he left, he would take what was his.

26

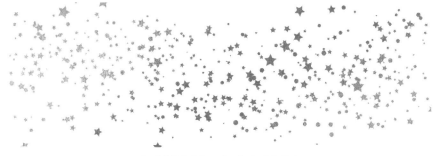

VIGILANCE

The Prize

Over her lifetime, she'd become adept at reading into silence. Threats and danger didn't always come from words, so the language she'd become proficient in was unspoken. Now *she* was silenced, but it allowed her to listen better. To observe more.

The air had shifted after the day those men had tried to drag her out. The quiet was deafening, both foreboding and foretelling. Despite her experience, she struggled to read this silence, to decipher the invisible words and that which lay ahead. Her own insecurities convinced her that despite the demonstrative golden shower, the unrivaled sex afterward, and Wes's attentiveness, they were considering getting rid of her.

Why wouldn't they? She knew to expect this. Everyone threw her away. She'd caused a problem, and now the problem needed to be eradicated.

No one liked being inconvenienced on that level.

It didn't matter that they continued to fuck her, continued to delight her with their caresses and tongues and cocks. Their double penetration of her—painful and frightening the first time—was becoming her favorite way to experience them. Her preferred position was sitting upright, straddling one man while the other was behind her, ramming up into her so hard she'd bounce on the cock of the man who held her. Her breasts moved vigorously, sending bolts of delight through her hard nipples. When Rogan was behind her, he'd collar her throat and angle her head back to look at him. If it was Wes, he preferred to hold on to them both, an all-encompassing embrace.

Being surrounded by them, filled by them, was an addiction.

She'd become their toy, their favorite game, and she loved being loved. Or at least fucked.

Wes delighted in making a mess. He'd giddily marked up the sheets and himself when her period returned after weeks. He lay back on the bed and declared, regarding his bloody cock, "It looks like you cut my dick off."

She'd raised her eyebrow and smiled as his dick resurrected itself before her eyes. His messiness was accompanied by affection and praise, the kind she'd remembered from before. With each encounter like this, her heart forgave him a little more.

Rogan was focused, either silent or accusatory. Their moment in the shower after he'd peed on her, when he'd been rough and tender simultaneously, had been fleeting. But now, he kissed her with honesty, ate her pussy with hunger, and fucked her with passion, even if that passion was expressed as anger. He wasn't playful, like Wes, but his intensity and focus were thrilling in a different way.

He tied her wrists to the headboard to ravish her. Any edging he attempted was foiled by Wes, so Rogan switched tactics, wringing from her as many orgasms as he could give her. She delighted in the ravishment. His tongue would swirl between her legs, thrusting into her, until she came. He wouldn't stop; he'd lick and nip and flick until she was exhausted and drenched in sweat, her muscles sore and her clit aching from overstimulation. Only when she was a rag doll would he fuck her, a triumphant gleam in his eyes.

Wes preferred to drag her over his face, his mouth working her to a frenzy while he stared up at her tits, pinching, twisting, and slapping as he ate her. Although he'd foil Rogan's edging, Wes's method was to take her to the edge and stop, blow on her clit to cool her down, then start the cycle over. It wasn't as torturous as Rogan's technique.

Different approaches, the same result: her body seizing with mind-blowing pleasure.

Why it mattered how they touched her, she didn't dissect. That was her entire purpose. She was here to service them; Rogan really, but Rogan was no longer being selfish when it came to her body. And they were including her in the act, ensuring her satisfaction, as if hers mattered more. Sometimes she wondered if they were competing to earn her orgasms and heart. Her *stupid* heart that latched on to any acts of kindness, even wrapped in sex—especially, really. A starving soul would walk over glass through fire for a taste of affection. Her needy and greedy soul would, at least. These men took care of her, and her neglected heart responded.

None of that helped her decipher the unspoken words or make sense of the long gazes the two men would exchange, communicating silently in the language she was typically so well-versed in. No, this silence deafened, and it wasn't a lexicon with which she was familiar.

Since the incident, another change had occurred. Wes had joined them for sex, and sometimes slept with them, for some time. But now, he was *around* more than he had been. She was never alone.

When Rogan left—she assumed for work—Wes would stay with her. Wes was usually inside her, making the most of having her to himself. If Wes was gone, then Rogan was home. Honestly, she was comforted by what she interpreted as greater protection. After she'd almost been taken and god knows what, they kept her in constant company.

Or maybe Rogan didn't trust her to roam freely, even if he'd given her permission to. Not alone, anyway. The permission was nice, but she preferred sitting on her bed in the corner. Normal people sat on sofas; she was not normal. Not anymore.

A couple of times, Rogan brought her with him when he left the building. He'd leash her—the collar having been replaced once the swelling had gone down—and walk seemingly aimlessly among the buildings. He took her to a picturesque park with a fountain, giving her a curious side-eye as she'd looked around.

If he'd expected her to marvel in the beauty of the place, she disappointed him. Beauty hid evil more times than not. Case in point: The park was pretty. The distant ocean was beautiful. The sun kissed her bare arms. Yet she was still a slave to the man who had her on a leash like his pet.

The two of them weren't objects of curiosity. It was odd considering their display days earlier. Children were running and shrieking, playing a game, like children did, either escaping their realities or oblivious to what went on around them. They looked innocent, but that was deceiving, all that which smiles hid. She knew about that firsthand, the masking.

There were others like her as well; perhaps that was why people rarely looked twice at her. The others weren't on leashes, but their demeanors, clothing, and blank expressions—as well as a couple with bruises—told their story. She would dart glances at them, then quickly look away if they made eye contact. It was bad enough, being what they were. Bearing witness to the plight of another was oddly embarrassing, like she was intruding on someone else's nightmare, as they had wandered into hers. They were powerless to stop it, so best to look away. She was an expert at that, too.

Her situation wasn't as bad as it could have been, and she took comfort in that. Given the circumstances, she was lucky. It was an odd word to use, but she could imagine worse. Though she didn't want to, for fear it would be a manifestation.

Rogan left her in the bed, one wrist secured to the headboard. He'd forgotten to remove it after he'd rolled over in the middle of the night and slid gently into her. His movements had been languid, savoring. She'd only been able to wrap one arm around him, holding him tightly as he drew himself slowly in and out. As if he wanted to take the time to learn what every stroke would feel like, rather than the furious pace he usually fucked her with.

She'd stared up at his shadowed face, into the dark glinting of his eyes, and had taken a tumble. The tenderness, the slow kisses, the *lovemaking*, had her falling. It was a dangerous emotion, but she couldn't help it. She liked to think that he was hers as much as she was his.

He stood in the darkened doorway, as if he didn't want to wake her. Her heart lurched at his thoughtfulness. Seconds later, another shadow appeared. Wes. Ah, the trade-off. He slapped Rogan on the shoulder as he passed by, moving into the bedroom. She closed her eyes before he could detect that she was awake.

"Fucking Ro," Wes cursed as he climbed into the bed and tugged on her restraint. He shifted away, and seconds later, there was a click. He removed her cuff, then he positioned her where he wanted her, spooning her, burying his face in her neck. After a few sniffs, he chuckled. "I love that he loves you so much he can't keep out of you."

Love. She hoped it wasn't just an expression. Her brain did mental gymnastics to both accept it and to guard her heart against the eventual letdown.

Down the hall, the water in the shower ran, and she immediately missed being under the spray with Rogan. It was comforting to stand in the warm stream with him, their hands gliding over one another, even if they didn't always fuck.

"Doll. Are you awake?" His whisper was soft against her ear as he nuzzled her.

It was unusual, his asking. Typically, he just took. More times than she could count, she'd been awakened by him thrusting into her, or his mouth sucking her clit. She wasn't complaining about it. His need called to her; she thrilled at his—and Rogan's—unbridled and wanton desire for her. During those moments, her fears of the communication to which she was not privy subsided.

But he'd asked, so he must have suspected she was awake.

She nodded.

"We're alone. He isn't here. You can talk to me." His tone was conspiratorial.

But he was here. He was in the next room. Even if he hadn't been, she didn't want to.

He sighed. "So well-behaved. I knew you would be perfect. You were perfect before, but now? My heart and cock ache for you more. I'm happy you're here, with us."

She frowned into the darkness, at odds with herself. He was expressing desire and affection, words he'd spoken to her before. Back then, they had catapulted her into giddy happiness. The sensation was reprised in her chest. Alongside it, though, was devastating heartbreak at the memories.

Why hadn't she been good enough for him then?

"The only thing I'd change is you being mine instead of his. I'd let you talk." He snuggled her closer, laughing quietly against her neck. "We'd still both be fucking you, though. Except for Narlina—the bitch—we share everything. Even if they'd offered, I didn't like who she became after she got married. But he loved her, and he's my best friend."

She deflated a bit. Being lumped in with *everything* took away from the joy that had engulfed her. She was aware of Wes and Rogan's physicality with one another—enticingly so—therefore it wasn't hard to imagine all that *everything* entailed.

"But I'm also a little sorry." He kissed her shoulder. "My impulse control sucks when it comes to you."

Her heart lurched to a halt before it sped forward. Although he'd tempered his regret, he was talking to her like it mattered, like she mattered. His affection was reminiscent of the way it had been before he'd brought her here. His words were easy, and the apology sounded sincere. Yet she didn't move.

"I'm not sorry for wanting you with me, but I'm sorry you had to go through that. It was the only way. And it's the only way I know how to get what I want. By taking it. But you're a fucking champ. I knew you would be; knew you could take what they dealt."

She glared into the empty hallway, scooting away from him.

"Where are you going?"

With a quick roll, she sat and moved farther away from his touch, stopping only when her back hit the headboard. She stared at him, her eyes accusing, her lips pressed tightly together.

Wes shifted, sitting too, studying her face. She hoped he could read everything she refused to say but blamed him for: she'd had a life, she was smart, she'd been happy with him, and she was so much more than what he'd made her become.

"Talk to me," he implored, his lips turned down in a concerned frown.

She jerked her chin upward defiantly, refusing. Her silence, she hoped, shrieked *this is what you did to me*. This was their reality now, and it was his fault. She wouldn't give him the satisfaction of her answer. Her precious voice. It would feel too much like forgiving him, and he didn't deserve absolution.

"I was afraid of losing you, of not being given permission to leave here, of never seeing you again." He sighed. "It doesn't help, but I didn't plan it. It was spontaneous."

The last part she couldn't bring herself to believe. But she would have preferred it if he just hadn't returned one day. She would have blamed herself, but *that* she was accustomed to: blaming herself for everything. It would have tracked, his disappearance from her life.

"Not that it matters here, but I swear I fell in love with you. So I had to keep you, right?"

Did she believe him? That he loved her? She wanted to. She wanted to be loved, to believe she was worthy of it. And the love she was accustomed to was accompanied by pain and vitriol. Maybe that was the only type of love he knew as well. Did she think it was romantic love, no matter what she wanted to believe? That which she'd felt for him at one time? No. He loved fucking her, the same way he and Rogan loved fucking one another, their use of the other for release. Did they enjoy it? Were they close? Yes, they were like brothers. Did she think one harbored romantic feelings toward the other? No. Maybe that's the way Wes felt about her, too. That would make more sense.

She was relieved that her voice had been taken from her. It saved her from having to respond, from being forced to talk to him. She didn't want to discuss the hurt he'd caused, the fear that was now her constant companion. She didn't want to forgive him even if it had brought her to Rogan, to the three of them.

Besides, he'd said it: love didn't matter here, even if her heart was determined to rebel against her mind so she could have it. Even if she was prone to create a twisted fairytale in her head.

So when he dragged her to him, then over him, his tongue spearing up into her, she ground against his mouth. She deserved to have her breasts squeezed, had earned his oral appreciation between her legs as she rode his face. She chased the high, eager for the moment her mind was set free and she was allowed to fly.

27

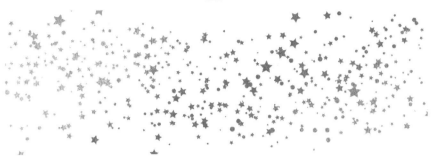

TRUTHS

Rogan

How is a population kept under control? They're controlled when they're given the reality they think they want, one that is easy to believe in. They're controlled when their concerns are justified away. That's exactly what Alan, Larry, and Trent presented to them. Where else does one receive free housing, beautiful weather, strict laws designed to keep them safe, and rewards and prizes? Above all, tell them they are free. Impress upon them that they can leave at any time, making a point to regularly highlight those who do leave. The same ones who always come back, like Wes and himself. Present the question and reinforce the narrative: they could leave, but why would they want to?

The trick was to make them want to stay. The bigger trick was to give them the illusion of a choice, because if one can choose their own destiny, then they're free.

The island residents were made of active employees and a few retired persons—those who had come years earlier to help establish the community. Several of the workers—the clinic's doctor, as an example—had been brought in as service slaves. There was no hierarchy for who could have a slave. Their landscaper had two service slaves: one for maintaining his household and one to assist him with the heavy lifting. Everyone had a purpose, with the exception of their few retirees. This, too, was necessary for the narrative: the rewards of lifelong devotion to the place.

Guests were never ending. The whirr of helicopters and the activity of boats at the dock on the other side of the island were constant. Some stayed a day, a week, a month, half the year. The duration of their visits varied. Their tastes even more so.

Then there were the others. His prize would be included in that category. She wasn't here because of her skill set; she was here because, well, because Wes had brought her here. But the service she provided was to fulfill a desire or fantasy. Sickeningly, some were bred, to keep the population of slaves going. Their offspring were then groomed for use, regardless of their age. What couldn't be grown, for lack of a better term, for the never-ending demands of the guests, had to be procured. None of these temporary inhabitants remained—read: *temporary*—nor did they leave.

The purpose of the island wasn't a secret, but denial is a powerful tool; if someone doesn't want to see something that is contrary to their beliefs, they won't. The narrative presented to them is the one they'll cling to. That was probably why some women stayed. That, and there weren't any prospects anywhere else. The education system on the island wasn't accredited, and indoctrination started on day one.

The mechanisms employed to exercise control over the small populace worked. Rogan, Wes, Narlina, and about twenty others had been the first generation born on the island. Their parents had established this twisted fantasyland for rich clients with deplorable habits.

The irony wasn't lost on Rogan. He was now a member of the club, the owner of a human. And he'd used her for his pleasure; both he and

Wes had. Curbing desires wasn't a rule here. No, desires were flaunted and celebrated. Case in point: he'd been gifted a woman and was cheered.

Rogan was one of a select, loyal few who had access to information. It was necessary to perform his job. The same went for Wes. Narlina may or may not understand the full extent of what happened on the island; she'd been selected as a child for Alan. She'd never told Rogan what kind of access she had. They'd never talked about it before, and he couldn't ask her now. Considering he was her only connection to the mainland, through his stories, he doubted she saw anything wrong with the way her life was playing out.

Rogan had wanted to leave after his second trip to the mainland. And he'd been so close. They'd been planning it for more than a year, he, Wes, and Narlina. *He* could always get away, once he'd earned enough cash—buy his way off the island. Others had done it. Narlina was another matter. She was married to the very person he wanted to escape. But they'd had a plan to remove their tracking devices and sneak her off the island.

Rogan knew information was provided sparingly; he was in charge of it. They were siloed. No one talked about the gaps in their understanding; their knowledge. Sometimes a person didn't want to know all the answers. It was an unspoken agreement that no one dug too deeply.

He was having a change of heart regarding the cone of silence, the complicity. All because of the quiet woman in the corner.

Previously, he'd only been interested in getting Narlina off the island undetected; had mapped a plan and path, given his job. He knew where the security cameras were, and more importantly, where they weren't. He knew angles at certain times of day. He knew how to jam signals.

Technically speaking, the island belonged to the United States. Therefore all the laws applied here. Not that it mattered. The residents either didn't know they were Americans, or they didn't care. Besides, no authority ever came here. That was part of Rogan's job: keeping them off radar, ensuring information didn't get off the island, and certainly keeping anything uncensored from making its way to the island. Money, privilege, and their own measures allowed the authorities to look away. The island wasn't suspect because they worked very hard not to *be* suspect.

He'd researched more while at work. What he'd discovered turned his blood cold. For a flicker of time, he was grateful to Narlina for the choice she'd made that day, for shattering his heart and dreams. Whether or not she knew it, she'd saved him. Saved them both.

Did she know? He didn't think so, based on their short conversation in the park and her duplicitous actions. If she'd had a better reason for her actions that day, she would have told him.

Because the truth he'd uncovered? No one other than the depraved and wealthy visitors voluntarily left the island. Dissenting voices disappeared under the guise of leaving—anyone who might upset the delicate balance necessary for keeping people captive. Even those who were seemingly free weren't. Though he supposed he'd known that.

In retrospect, suspicion should have been roused when previous occupants who had chosen to leave and reside on the mainland never visited, never contacted the families they'd left on the island. Of course, the dead don't call.

When Rogan quietly relayed his findings, Wes didn't look surprised.

"You knew," Rogan accused. "You knew, and you were willing to let me walk to my death."

"Do you think I'd let that happen?"

"How would you have prevented it?"

He looked uneasy, the man he'd thought a friend, a confidant. "Sometimes my work includes disbursement of property."

Rogan took a solid step backward, his chest tightening in shock. "Jesus Christ." How could he not have known? Of course, survival on this island depended on secrets. He knew there was a great deal of information most of the people there were unaware of. But Wes hadn't told him any of this. Only then did reality sink in. "Our mothers."

"That wasn't me. I was a kid then."

Had they ever been kids? Had there been a time when they were innocent?

"It's the part of my job I don't like," he admitted. "But you weren't leaving like the others. You were sneaking, with Narlina."

"I was going to buy my way out of here. They would have known." Rather than buying a person's own freedom or paying for escape, it was presented as a traveler's fee; the cost of taking one of the boats or a helicopter. Rogan knew seven who had waved goodbye. The boats or helicopter came back empty, as they should have. No suitcases or packed food in tow. But according to what Wes was saying, the passengers never made it to the mainland. Or they did, but they didn't get far.

"I would have been in charge of"—Wes made a face—"disposal." He looked sheepish, scratching the back of his neck. "You know I wouldn't have."

Rogan considered his friend differently, for the first time not certain if he was someone he could trust. How could he not have doubts?

"I'd never do anything to hurt you, Ro. Certainly not her." He was referring to his doll. "I'd fucking take myself out first."

His words were emphatic. A strange level of intensity for a man who had committed greater crimes against the woman.

Rogan hoped his friend meant it. Hoped he'd never need to test Wes's sincerity in that.

28

AFFECTION
The Prize

"*Am I pretty, momma?*" *She posed in front of the large bathroom mirror, waiting in anticipation of the assurance that the kids at school, on the TV, received from their mothers. She wanted the acceptance, the admission that she was, indeed, a pretty child, the indication of love the response would bring. The feeling of being valued.*

"No." The answer came easily. "You'll never be pretty as long as you're fat."

She was nine. The answer should have come easily. But for her mother, truth was more important than feelings. She'd been crushed, her little heart devastated, which, in retrospect, she found odd. Nothing in her young life should have given her the expectation that the answer would have been different. But a child's need was never ending. Or maybe it was just her. Hugs and expressions of love were uncommon. Even so, it shouldn't have been hard to let a little girl think she was pretty, even if she wasn't.

So, was she pretty? No. Certainly not a child a mother could love, especially while an ounce—or more—of fat was on her. She'd always had the pouch and always would—if being a sex slave didn't rid her of it, nothing would.

Wes had told her *before* that he liked it. He'd lay his head on her abdomen, insisting he liked the softness of her belly. And maybe he'd been telling the truth, because it hadn't deterred either of them from fucking her to soreness.

But that was her purpose.

In the past, she'd take selfies to the point of looking narcissistic or vain. But in reality, she had only been searching for signs of beauty, what others saw, what her mother hadn't.

Wes had told her she was beautiful; Wes was a liar.

For the few weeks they had been a normal couple, she had seen herself as pretty, had viewed herself through his eyes. He'd given her confidence. Shown her love. Acceptance. Everything she'd wanted. Then he'd destroyed it all.

She pinched at the fat on her abdomen, dimpling her skin. Rogan fed her. She was also allowed to cook sometimes. Other than her two-day refusal to eat the oatmeal, she hadn't gone hungry. Her initial captivity and deprivation hadn't moved the stubborn pudge. Her stress and recent sexual activities weren't enough to burn this from her. The soreness and swelling of her throat after she'd been strangled hadn't prevented consumption. Walks weren't regular, so the exercise wasn't beneficial.

"Fuck."

His tortured whisper caught her attention. Lowering her t-shirt, she considered him. He sat on the sofa in front of a television that replayed a show she'd seen playing days ago, a benign sitcom. Rogan dropped his head back onto the top cushions, defeated, his hand falling to his side, his phone loose in his grasp.

He'd been distracted more than usual. It was clear he was planning something—he and Wes—and his frustrations had shifted more than once in recent days. He almost appeared desperate as he stared up at the ceiling, like he wanted to cry.

A dormant sensation poked at her. The urge to comfort. After the horrors she'd been through, that was still inside her. It made her feel human; it also made her more aware of her imprisonment, but she shoved that aside. Instead, she focused on the part of her that was, for a moment, normal.

She slowly left her bed. He'd allowed her to move around, but each time she tested the boundary, she still felt as though she needed permission. However, this was an action she was willing to be rebuked for. She wanted to feed her humanity.

She crawled to him, her movement catching his attention. He rolled his head on the cushions and watched her, his expression curious. She hesitated, but when he didn't command her back to the corner, she continued.

The first time she'd crawled across the floor, everything in her had rebelled at the debasement, the intent to humiliate. She'd crawled a few times since—his pet—but not in a sexual manner. This time, she was willing. Sure, she could stand and walk over to him, but he needed this from her, and she was willing to give it.

Her movements were deliberate. In her mind's eye, she was slinking forward in a sultry manner. And from the way his Adam's apple bobbed in a hard swallow, it was clear he appreciated it.

When she sidled up to him, she slipped between his legs and lay her head on his thigh. Her body was taut with tension, anticipating his response to the contact. The only sounds other than inane chatter from the television were their breaths.

Only a moment later, he rested his hand on her head. Lightly, at first, but then he committed, stroking her dark hair. Her heart nearly exploded, her body flushing with heat. It wasn't desire; it was affection, given and taken. The emotions were overpowering, that he would give this to her; of course, she had given it to him first. But it didn't matter. For twenty minutes, she was allowed to feel useful, to provide comfort, she hoped.

When he took a handful of her hair and tilted her head back, he wore a tender smile. The first he'd ever given her. It was full of appreciation. He was looking at her—*her*—for the first time since their moment in the shower. He stroked a finger along her cheek.

The front of his sweatpants tented slowly as his cock hardened. Pride burst through her. After her morose thoughts moments ago, this was evidence that he wanted her. She was eager to oblige.

With her attention fixed on his face, she lowered his waistband, his erection springing free. Shifting onto her knees, she stroked him, enjoying how his eyelids fluttered. They'd been in similar positions before, usually with Wes accompanying them, and Rogan had fucked her mouth.

This was different. She was taking him, quietly and reverently. Leaning forward, she sucked one of his balls into her mouth. His jolt and moan, the tightening of his fingers in her hair, propelled her. She loved making him squirm; she didn't often get the opportunity. So she took her time, one ball at a time. Then she licked up his dick. Her hand took over massaging his balls, and when they moved, satisfaction spiked through her.

In truth, when she freely gave it, she enjoyed sucking and licking a man's hard cock, tonguing his testicles, making him buck and whimper the way he and Wes made her writhe and gasp. She owned him, and for these few sweet minutes, he wanted to be owned by her.

She deep-throated him with purpose then, glancing up at his face as she took him in as deep as she could. He was watching her back, watching his dick disappear into her mouth. His breathing was labored now, and his thighs were twitching. He jerked upward a couple of times, but he mostly let her take charge as he enjoyed her attention.

Their eyes met, and she almost stopped. The shock hit so hard, hit them both. He looked as stunned as she. For that moment, they were equals, taking and giving pleasure without being defined by the trappings of their surroundings. Like the shower, but more intense. Intentional.

He burst into her mouth, his head dropping back, and she drank him down. He came so much she gagged a little, but she managed. And she licked away what spilled out.

"Fuck." This time when that word slipped from his lips, he didn't sound despondent or frustrated. His tone was one of appreciation, pleasure.

She gingerly tucked him back into his pants, watching him. His chest rose and fell as he caught his breath. His fingers in her hair relaxed and started stroking again. Content, she lay her head back down on his thigh. He let her stay there through the next bland sitcom.

When he finally spoke, continuing to stroke her hair, his voice was soft, gentle. "I've seen you looking at the bookshelf. If you want to read them, that's what they're here for."

She should feign indifference, hide how much his words affected her. Attachment was used as a tool of manipulation; it wasn't in her best interest to get excited about anything. But the truth was, he couldn't have given her a better gift. Lifting her head from his thigh, she beamed at him.

29

SUBMISSION

Rogan

Maybe she was bitter deep down, but if so, she didn't display it. Not toward him, anyway. She desired the basics: affection, kindness, and a connection. The same things most humans wanted. Her brown eyes watched him, looking for—craving—the tidbits of kindness he dropped on her, the sex aside. And the appreciation that burst from her in those small moments made him waver.

She wanted to please him. Not because of her circumstance—at least not entirely—but because it resulted in his smile, his attention. She didn't mind, not that he could tell, the way he treated her like a pet: collar, leash for walks, bowl of water beside her dog bed. He wouldn't go so far as to say she acted like a dog, beyond what she was forced to do, but her yearning for a soft stroke of her hair wasn't unlike that of Ruff. His dog had sensed his moods and offered comfort, too. And the small gestures helped. Just as her small gestures had for those calming moments.

And any attention he gave her was lapped up, just as it had been with Ruff.

She was smart. He'd noticed that early on. When he'd given her permission to take a book, her face had lit up. Disbelief collided with gratefulness as she'd surveyed him, but he'd seen something else, too. He'd seen a glimpse into who she may have once been, an intelligent light reflecting in her eyes, a spark rekindled. It nearly undid him again.

She'd already undone him with her perfect mouth, but the look kickstarted something in him he hadn't known he'd needed, wanted. An emotion he didn't know he was capable of when it came to her. When their eyes had met, his cock sliding into her mouth, the connection was transportive. He could imagine a world beyond this place. One that included *her*.

It was shocking. He hadn't let himself think about what would happen if they got away, instead focusing on getting them to that point. He'd worry about the after if they made it. But after that searing exchange, he was certain he wanted her with him. Of her own will. It was a fucking revelation.

Narlina had loved him, but she hadn't appreciated all he'd done for her. She'd taken everything he gave her for granted. Even so, he'd wanted to do it for her anyway. He hadn't had a real comparison before, but now he could very clearly see the differences between entitled appreciation and genuine gratefulness.

His pet was a damn fine cook, too. He didn't have a lot of options, but on the few occasions he'd instructed her to prepare their meals, her concoctions had been top-notch. He'd found himself imagining where she'd learned the skill. Had she done it professionally? Quickly, he'd catch himself and force his musings away. Whatever she'd been before, that life was gone.

She was now in her corner with a book. The faraway look on her face was dreamlike rather than zoned out, like it so often had been. She was somewhere else, someone else, far away from this island. Relaxed. Free.

He caught himself smiling. He *liked* her, his prize. Not only was she fucking beautiful—thank you, Wes, for having good taste—but she was intriguing. He hated that he liked her, like he was losing something in admitting it. But this tiny glimpse into her personality warmed his heart. He wanted to fuck her right now, but he didn't want to take her tiny escape away from her.

Wes would laugh at him, then high-five him. He'd ask why it had taken him so long to see what he'd seen. In reality, Rogan had seen her more clearly with less information than Wes had been given. Because Wes had encountered her when she was... herself. If this shackled woman could demand so much of his attention, need, and desire, then yeah, Rogan was beginning to understand how Wes, who'd known the woman she'd been, was determined to have her with him all the time.

A knock interrupted his lazy perusal of her. His heart leaped with dread. The fist was heavy, meaning it wasn't Wes. Before he could make a move to answer it, however, the door swung open.

Alan didn't look like a mastermind, nor did he look cruel. Not even intimidating. After all, his name was Alan. He wasn't bulky—he was scrawny, actually—compared to other men. On the mainland, he would easily be confused with a stereotypical accountant. Maybe he'd been trained as an accountant; after all, he was like the executive director of this place.

His ego was the largest thing about him. And his power, nefarious as it was. He held it all. No one crossed Alan. He wasn't openly threatening, but he dealt quickly with those who broke the rules, like the men who'd tried to take his prize. Alan had allowed and approved instant justice for such offenses.

Maybe that's how he kept his benevolent reputation, by letting others deal out justice while he doled out prizes. But Rogan's eyes had been opened to the depths of the man's depravity when he'd started grooming Narlina. The more Rogan learned, the more his intense dislike of this man grew.

Had he been loyal to Alan, to this island and its occupants? Yes, he'd been as indoctrinated as everyone else here. But somewhere along the way, the rose-colored glasses had slipped off, and leaving this place had become his priority. But there was a saying: keep your friends close, but your enemies closer. Until the moment Alan crossed this threshold, Rogan had been in the man's good graces.

This visit told him the favoritism was tarnished. An unannounced late-night visit from Alan didn't bode well. If it had to do with the men Rogan had harmed, it would have been handled in public. He'd heard rumors of other late-night visits, but none that were ever substantiated. Who would risk it by gossiping outright? And there had been that moment at the beach; his stare, his interest. Between that and his own public claiming of her, he should be more surprised it'd taken this long for Alan to visit.

Rogan stared evenly at the older man as he shut the door.

Alan's attention shifted to her, and Rogan followed his line of sight. Her book was gone, and her hands were folded on her lap as she stared back. Even from the kitchen, the fear and wariness in her eyes were clear. She wouldn't know who he was, but she was smart enough to read the tension that descended upon them.

Alan raised an eyebrow at him. "One of our best trainers is dead. I wanted to see for myself how a slave could rouse such..." He tilted his head, as if he were considering his words. Rogan wasn't fooled. The man had arrived with a script. "Devotion."

Yes, this was a lesson. A comeuppance. Rogan wouldn't let his worry show. He wasn't worried for himself; he was concerned about what would become of her. *Gifts weren't revocable*, but who knew why a slave suddenly disappeared or met with an untimely tragedy? Rogan didn't want to know whether those rumors were true.

In his periphery, she turned toward Rogan. He fought every instinct screaming at him to look at her. If he did, he'd give this man more ammunition. "All due respect, I'm not sorry for their loss. I'll defend what's mine."

Alan hummed. "'All due respect' is a polite way of telling me to go fuck myself. I think there's a disconnect here."

Rogan frowned. His sense of foreboding was increasing by the second. "That's not how I meant it. What disconnect?"

The man took a deep breath, then let it out slowly, a demonstration of feigned patience, tolerance. "It's expected of her to be devoted to you. To all of us. That's her purpose. Her body belongs to you, to me. It's your care toward her that's troubling. Your…" His gaze hardened. "Affection. Some might call it compassion. In some circumstances, that's a valued trait. But when it comes to a slave, it's dangerous. And catching."

"Catching?"

"A plague. A weakness."

Rogan's stomach churned, and panic seeped into his veins.

"Emotions cripple us. Empathy breeds dissent." Alan's eyes slid back to the corner. "She's a tool. I'll demonstrate." He gestured. "On her feet."

Rogan looked at her, meeting wide, scared eyes. She might not know Alan's title, but based on her expression, she'd interpreted Alan's words accurately. And she understood that Rogan was not in control of this situation. Reluctantly, he jerked his chin and held out his hand to her.

She scrambled to her feet while attempting to hold the hem of his shirt down. It was a strangely modest gesture for a sex slave. Across the room, Alan was smirking. Rogan's stomach bottomed out.

She flew to him, as if afraid that she would be snatched back at any moment, and grasped his hand. He pulled her to him, wrapping his arm around her. She was shaking, anticipating what was about to happen. Holding her to him might not have been the best choice—tipping his hand, although it was already tipped—but if his arm around her was any comfort or conciliation to her, he wanted to provide it.

As Alan approached them, Rogan managed to control himself enough not to shove her behind him, out of the man's reach. No matter how he tried to protect her—and his need to do so was overwhelming—he wouldn't prevail.

Another flip of Alan's wrist accompanied his words. "Clothes off."

Her body went rigid, and she pulled in a sharp breath. She pressed harder against him, like he could save her. But he couldn't save her from this. Being fucked was her purpose. He despised it, but in order to survive this moment, she'd have to submit. There was no way he could kill this man like he'd killed the other one.

This man was untouchable. And her body *was* touchable.

Rogan turned her to face him and stared into her scared brown eyes, eyes that pleaded with him for help, hoping he could convey to her that he wouldn't leave her alone. His presence wouldn't matter in the grander scheme of things, but if she had to endure this, he would suffer too. He would bear witness.

The fear and betrayal he saw as he regarded her would haunt him. He wanted to rail, make her understand that he wasn't betraying her—a *sex slave*—as he lifted the shirt over her head. He held her gaze as he dropped the article of clothing. She was trembling. He stepped up to her and cupped her face between his hands.

"Think rationally, Rogan. She might belong to you, but she's a whore for us all. Whores can't love. They don't feel."

Rogan's heart dropped right out of his body. She felt; her horror was on par with his own. "She's a victim." It was the truth. A victim of Wes, of himself, of the place.

"Sluts aren't victims. But you, boy, pose a danger because of your deferential treatment of a disposable product. Heed your lesson."

He continued to hold her face between his hands, to memorize every detail of the desperate plea written there. He wanted to defend her, to argue that she wasn't a product. But that would be playing into his hands. In the quiet, the only sound was their breathing, then the lowering of Alan's zipper.

Her eyes widened; she shifted toward Rogan, still delusional enough to think he could stop what was about to happen. He hoped she could take solace knowing she wouldn't be forced to look her rapist in the face.

He didn't take his focus off her as her hips jerked backward, being positioned. Tears leaped to her eyes, creating a hairline fracture in his heart. He angled in and brushed his lips along hers. She let out a small sound as the man behind her spat. She jerked as the sound of a palm striking flesh rent the air.

Placing his lips against her ear, he whispered, "It's only me and Wes, pet. We have you."

She jolted, propelling herself toward him as though she could escape through him. Her action was accompanied by a short scream. Her fingers dug into his shirt.

Slipping his hands from her face, he grasped the back of her neck and pulled her to him. Looking down the length of her back—because he sure as shit wasn't going to look Alan in the face, even as the man's rancid breath hit him with each pant—he tightened his hold on the back of her head, pressing her harder against him.

Her ass. Alan was fucking her ass, with nothing more than his spit to force his way in. And he wasn't being gentle; he'd filled her completely and was jerking furiously.

She attempted to move away, to flee, to raise up on her toes. A diabolical laugh echoed through the apartment. "Fight me, yes; it makes it so much better."

Rage tore through him: at himself, at the man taking from her, taking from him. He was disgusted by his powerlessness. His anger landed on Narlina. She'd wanted him here, wanted him as subjugated as the whimpering, crying woman in his arms. In that moment, the full realization of how owned he was crashed down on him.

Because he was letting this happen. He had no choice. They were all puppets on precarious strings.

Her tears soaked his shirt. Warm liquid hit his bare foot. Alan hadn't come yet. His disgusting grunts still mingled with her cries. She hadn't lost control of her bowels; there was no hot stream running down the front of him. Moving his foot slightly, he looked.

Blood. She was bleeding.

She would be bitter now, and she had every right to be. As much as he'd hated her, he never wanted something so horrific for her. But that meant nothing. He was holding her while it happened. He may as well be the one hurting her.

30

REVICTIMIZATION
The Prize

Over time, their threesome had become a unit. For the first time since she stepped onto that yacht, she'd begun to feel a semblance of safety. That didn't mean she didn't maintain her vigilance. She wasn't *safe*—nothing about her situation was actually safe—but with Rogan and Wes, she felt cherished.

Was it a sustainable relationship? Of course not. But she refused to think beyond the present. The reality that the only way off this island for her would be through death—and odds were sooner rather than later—was always in the back of her mind. But she suspended her disbelief like the champ Wes had called her and fooled herself most nights when she was sandwiched between them, clinging to the fantasy that her demise wasn't close. And she loved the press of their hard bodies against her, even when she'd turn into a furnace from their joint body heat. She suffered the discomfort. It was small in comparison to being cool and alone.

Wes slept with them most nights. When he was in the bed, she wasn't shackled by one wrist to the headpost. She was beginning to think that

Rogan did it not because he didn't trust her not to kill him in the middle of the night, but because he liked the aesthetic. Or because she'd tried to escape once. More likely, it was because he'd been betrayed once, and letting her go wasn't an option. More than anything, that was what she'd hoped: *he couldn't let her go.*

When they did shackle both her wrists, it served their purpose for other activities. She was thrilled when they restrained her. She'd orgasmed the hardest she ever had when both men tongued her at the same time. They lay wrapped around each other, her legs spread far apart to accommodate them both. They'd flicked their tongues over her clit, lapping up her wetness. She'd been transported, looking down the length of her body to these two men parrying with her clit.

They were intent, focused. As she fought to maintain her silence, she swore Rogan smiled. His smile was golden. His dark eyes lifted to hers. She would do anything for the praise she saw there.

Because she was so focused on his eyes, she wasn't sure whose fingers plunged into her and finger-fucked her with force. But that move was enough to push her over the brink. Watching her as intently as he had been, or simply by sensing it, as her body froze in the instant before it burst apart, Rogan shoved Wes away, claiming her clit for his own, sucking and biting.

How she didn't scream out loud, she didn't know. But she wasn't quiet, either; it was impossible. Moans and muffled cries escaped her, a flash of heat overtaking her.

Soar, soar, soar. He gave her wings and let her fly. Wes watched proudly; she wasn't sure which of them earned that look from him. It could have been both of them. As she fell back to earth, though, Rogan raised up and sank into her. Wes took her mouth. Filled with them, she flew once more.

She loved the sex, but just as valuable was Wes's easy-going nature. He made her laugh, surprising her with a joke made at Rogan's expense, which she stifled behind a hand. In these moments, she remembered the man who'd charmed her into danger. And here with them now, protected and accepted, her heart began to heal. Their bodies fed her. She belonged to them. She *belonged*.

Despite her early introduction to sex, she hadn't become a textbook case of a person who became promiscuous when she was older. She saw herself as fat and unlovable; that mindset didn't translate to taking on many partners. Maybe it was denial, dissociation, or compartmentalizing—slap any label on it—but she wanted these men, wanted the way they touched her. Her pillow talk with Wes, from before, was playing out. She wanted this. Only, not like *this*.

Burgeoning relationship or not, Rogan hadn't returned her voice to her. It wasn't a pressing need; it hadn't felt like a burden. She'd been told her entire life what her reality was: what she should hear, or experience. In essence, she'd had no voice long before Rogan had taken it from her.

Whatever semblance of safety and protection she'd felt, however, was torn away when the strange man had used her in ways reminiscent of her days in the cage. No, worse, and that was one heck of an admission, that she'd have preferred rape one way over the other. But she did, because they hadn't been allowed to damage her the same way. No blood, no tearing in that dank, evil space. The stranger's actions had done more to rip away her shaky acceptance in cruel, painful moments than the caged room had.

Because in that blacked-out space, she could fantasize about escaping, really escaping. With Wes and Rogan, she could pretend there was normalcy, even if it was one far different from what she'd ever imagined. They weren't violent with her, didn't beat her, didn't share her beyond the two of them. She'd been theirs alone.

That had been her state of mind before it happened. When she'd looked into Rogan's tortured gaze as she'd been violated, she saw the limits of his willingness to protect her. Not even his whispered assurances—*it'll be over soon*—and gentle cleaning of her after the monster left could keep her from trembling. Her soreness, she would get over, and it was clear he was bothered by his inability to take care of her. She emitted choked sobs to maintain her silence, even as he encouraged her to let it out. But clinging to something familiar had been necessary. And if she opened her mouth, she wouldn't stop screaming.

The irony didn't escape her. She'd been craving his arms around her for weeks, and the moment she was in them, he had held her as another man brutalized her.

The return of her reality blasted through her, forcing her to face all those things she had wanted to will away: She was property. She was expendable. She was breakable. All the traumas she'd endured as a child, those rapes, were reprised. Somehow, this one hurt worse. Back then, she'd had no one to care for her. But now, Rogan had pretended to care for her, and she'd fallen for it. The betrayal sliced deeper than what that man had done to her.

The man's parting words had been a warning to Rogan and a threat—or a promise, depending on perspective—to her. He'd sneeringly mocked Rogan's deferential treatment of her (it hadn't felt deferential at the time). "You're coddling a goddamn whore whose only purpose is to provide holes to fuck and to make you feel like a god." To break Rogan of his *affection*, Alan announced that her body would be at *his* disposal.

If that happened again—or worse—she would finally break apart. There would be no hope left. Her protector wouldn't shield her; he could only be a witness.

And she wasn't a champ.

They may not have created her, but they would be the ones who finally destroyed her. She'd known this from the beginning. Now it was coming to fruition.

The survivor in her no longer wished to fight this fight. Succumbing, not fighting back, would prompt others to blame her for being weak. But weakness hadn't gotten her to this point. This was fucking hard.

31

FLIPPED

Rogan

Wes had been furious about her rape. Rogan gave him a side-eye. Hadn't Wes been the one to force her to take his cock into her mouth on that first night? Hadn't he then tried to drop her on Rogan's dick? Wasn't Wes responsible for her presence here in the first place?

His friend climbed into the bed with her and held her, rocking her. He promised her things he could never follow through on: Revenge. Protection.

Her eyes were vacant, like she'd gone deep inside and didn't plan on returning. Maybe she didn't. He couldn't blame her.

After the assault, when he'd tried to take care of her, guilt had slammed into him like a sledgehammer. He contemplated whether his presence—the way he'd held her through the attack—had anchored her in the moment. As he'd wiped away the blood and cum streaming down the backs of her legs, he pondered if she'd been more aware of what was happening to her because he wouldn't let her go. Could she have disappeared inside her mind while her body was being torn into if he hadn't been talking to her? Telling her it would be over soon?

He'd never told her it would be okay. That was one lie he knew he couldn't tell. It was a lie Wes kept repeating. "You're gonna be okay, baby doll. Everything is going to be all right."

The words had earned his friend another side-eye. But words didn't matter. His pet, Wes's doll, was beyond hearing. Was this how she'd endured the training? Disappearing inside her mind? But she'd been dropped at his feet clear-eyed, scared but present.

He could demand her presence now, her attention, but he wouldn't. She deserved to crawl into whichever shell she needed to recover. He wanted to join her there, but he wasn't sure he would be welcome.

So he let Wes fuss over her. It wouldn't matter. Something in her had shattered. After being stolen, surviving the training, and almost being taken a second time, this had decimated her. She'd just started to lean into the life she had here with him and Wes. He liked to think she was content. Not happy, exactly, but at least not constantly afraid.

Until one man wrecked her. That was a lie: two men. The one who had raped her and the one who had held her through it.

• • • • ● • ● • • •

Rogan prepared sandwiches for the three of them. She wasn't eating very much, but she was drinking. The first time he'd escorted her to the bathroom afterward, he'd shifted away to give her privacy. Her narrowed glance had accused him when he did so, so he'd stopped and remained in the doorway. Confused.

After bathing her that night, he'd helped her into a pair of sweatpants, hoping she would feel less vulnerable. It never occurred to him before that she would feel exposed. Fucked up time to be contemplating that. So he was perplexed by what he read as her desire for him to stay in the bathroom with her. Was it a form of protection? Wasn't she bearing the reminders that his protection was worthless?

He was beginning to not only sympathize with her, but to empathize. He and Wes had asked her more than once to tell them what she needed, but her glossy-eyed look was their only answer. He was surprised by how much he cared, how much her blank expression bothered him. He hadn't realized how much she meant to him before the night he couldn't do a damn thing to save her.

Or how much he wanted to see the expression he'd gotten from her when he'd offered her something as simple as a book.

Of course, it was fucked up to even consider how to shield a sex slave. But he had never really seen her as that. A pet, yes. An initially unwanted one, at that. Her horror, at being owned, matched his repulsion to owning.

A light rap came on the door. Rogan glared at it, the jolt of fear pissing him off. But the knock hadn't been heavy. So he called out, giving permission to enter, even though the door was opening. He remained at the kitchen island, grinding his teeth. Personal boundaries weren't respected on an island like this, not when Alan—or his wife—wanted an audience. Or to fuck what belonged to someone else.

Narlina slipped into the apartment, looking over her shoulder, as though her visit was clandestine. She knew it wasn't. There were cameras everywhere. His apartment had never been their safe haven because of it.

"What do you want?" His voice was harsh. Unfeeling. He no longer felt anything for her.

She closed the door and leaned back against it. She wore another blue sheath gown that highlighted her alabaster skin and brilliant blue eyes. "Rogan." Her tone was one of sorrowful appeal, as though saying his name in that manner would remind him of what they'd once meant to one another.

He shook his head, dropping his attention to the sandwiches in front of him. When he was a kid, he liked them cut into squares, so he set about doing so, for his pet. Maybe she'd be more inclined to eat smaller portions.

"Rogan, please listen to me." Her voice was a soft, whispered plea.

He continued to ignore her. Would his pet like potato chips? He and Wes had tried tempting her with many foods: ice cream, cookies. Wes swore she had a sweet tooth, but they hadn't found a single thing that enticed her yet. Maybe chips would.

"I've made a mess of everything. I know it."

At least she was being honest. He lifted hard eyes to her.

It hadn't been an invitation for her to continue talking, but she did so anyway.

"I was scared. I told you I was scared. There's no way he would let me go." Her tone was hushed, as though she was afraid *he* could hear her. "He doesn't let anyone go."

That was a truth he'd learned on his own, and Wes had confirmed it. But... "Why are you only telling me this now?"

She sagged in relief. Because he'd spoken to her, he supposed. Moving into the room, she affected a demure expression. "I should have trusted you. If anyone could get away from here, it would be you. But it was a last-minute decision to pull the other lever."

So much for being honest. But he was intrigued. She was playing another game, and he wanted to know what it was. Knowledge was power. It was also too coincidental for her to show up almost on the heels of her husband's visit.

"Last minute." He huffed. "How was a human placed in the other chute? You said both would contain money."

"I... I wanted it to look real. So that no one would question it."

"How many people have questioned you or Alan? Ever? At least questioned and then lived?"

She sighed, the sound one of pure frustration. "You're questioning me now."

He motioned between them with the knife. "We were best friends before we were lovers. I get to question why you betrayed me. And I get to question why you're here now, claiming you made a mistake."

"*Were*?" Her tone and her expression were laced with pain, as if she were wounded by that one word.

He barked out a laugh. "Do you see a future for us?"

"Yes, it's possible. I'm still me, Ro. I was wrong to do what I did. I was scared." Her voice dropped back into a whisper. "But I'm *more* scared now."

"It's too late for you to realize that."

She shook her head. "I don't think it is."

Rogan tilted his head, his guard rising higher. "What do you mean?"

"Come on, I know you. You aren't satisfied with a whore. Content, maybe, depending on her skills."

"Calling her a whore assumes she's a willing participant. She's not. Don't fucking call her that." He jabbed, "She didn't sell her soul for comfort, all the while betraying those who *did* love her."

"I didn't—"

"Yes, you did." He swiped the air with his hand, signaling the end of the debate. He wouldn't tolerate his pet being degraded by a disloyal bitch. He was the only one who could call his prize names. She loved it from him.

Not even Wes would be allowed, not that he would. Their approaches to her were different, complementary; they balanced each other.

Narlina huffed, perusing the space. She glanced toward the darkened hallway, and her blue eyes flared with jealousy. After all, if his prize wasn't in the front room, then she was in his bedroom. And based on her look of distaste, the bedroom equated to sex. Not rest, not recuperation after her husband had gone on a raping spree.

"What do you want, Narlina?"

She schooled herself, lifting her chin and smoothing the front of her skirt. How had he not noticed until now how cold her face was? Wes would tell him he had been pussy whipped. Seeing her now, he had to agree.

"He wants a baby."

Rogan scoffed.

"I can't, Rogan. I mean, I can have babies, but..." Her eyes filled with tears and genuine fear. "I don't want to raise a baby here. I don't want *his* baby."

Her enunciation, he supposed, was to make him think that she wanted Rogan's baby.

He kept his expression neutral. "There isn't anything I can do about that."

There was a flash of frustrated anger in her eyes. She wasn't getting her way like she was accustomed to. He wasn't doing everything in his power to make her happy, to see to her needs as he always had, and she didn't know how to deal with that.

"I know you're planning something."

The certainty in her voice made him laugh. Shaking his head, he looked down at the sandwiches again. But damn, she did know him. He should have been prepared for this. He denied it, of course. "With what money, love?" The moniker was to taunt.

"That won't stop you."

"I appreciate your confidence in me, but I'm stuck here. It's what you wanted."

Narlina stepped closer to the bar separating them. "When you go, take me with you."

"Like I said, it's too late for regrets, babe. I've been hobbled. But thank you for my pet so I won't get lonely. I am more than pleased with her."

The fire flared again. She really hated that he had his prize. Narlina's hatred only stoked his affection for his dark-haired beauty.

"Let me put it to you this way: I will watch every move you make. I know you're planning an escape, as sure as I know my own name." Placing her hands on the bar top, she leaned forward. "You take me, or you don't go. I can chain you like that bitch."

Rogan stared back at her. He fought the urge to defend his prize, to remind her again that she was the one who had deposited the golden woman at his feet—it no longer mattered that Narlina hadn't known what she was delivering, because she hadn't provided their future, their escape.

No, instead of arguing with her, he stared at her, confused. How the hell didn't she know that he was already chained when she's the one who'd secured the lock?

32

MASKING
The Prize

Wes lurked in the hallway, listening. She'd padded from the bedroom behind him, not wanting to be left alone. Not after the man's visit. When he halted, though, so did she.

That's when the conversation in the kitchen broke through the fog she'd been enshrouded in. Some of it was too quiet to hear, but she heard Rogan's acceptance of the unknown proposal the woman had made.

Minutes later, the door opened and closed. Wes dropped his head, shook it, then pushed off the wall and walked into the front room. She sidled closer, leaving the doorway, but she hadn't needed to. Wes was yelling.

"What the fuck are you doing showing your hand like that? How do you know she won't hightail it back to Alan and tell him?"

"Not now," came Rogan's weary response. "Take these sandwiches to—"

The sound of glass shattering startled her, making her jump and sending her heart racing.

"Wes!"

"You could be a dead man in an hour. We could all be dead in an hour."

Her heart lurched. Strangely, the dread that consumed her wasn't for herself, but for them.

"No, I won't be. She's getting what she wants. When I go, she goes with me."

Rejection rocked through her. Of course, when given the choice between a nobody like herself and the woman he'd cried over that first night, he would choose his first love—his only love, as far as she knew.

She was disposable. The man had said it. They would dispose of her.

Turning, she retraced her steps to the bed the three of them shared. Despite his light, comforting caresses and interspersed apologies, she was nothing to him. Whatever the men were planning, she wasn't a part of it; her paranoia from weeks before came back to her. She would be left behind, left to the mercies of these people. It wasn't ideal, her current situation, but she'd found momentary happiness, a sense of belonging. She felt genuine affection for the first time in a long time.

But it followed the pattern she should have anticipated. This was how it always went. How no one in her life came through for her. She was used and forgotten. She rushed across emotional boundaries because she didn't know where the lines were, and it only served to hurt her even more.

After the night Narlina appeared, she listened and watched them plan. They'd done it many times before, but there was an urgency now. Not that she could talk, but when the time came, she wouldn't tell anyone what she was witnessing. Considering everything, these men had been good to her. And she was very good at keeping secrets. Her heart was loyal, even if theirs weren't.

Each day that passed was a torment. She saw no indication of them including her, except in bed. After hearing what she had in the hall, her survival instinct kicked in, anything to ingratiate herself to them. Wes was easier to cuddle up with, kiss, stroke. He'd been taken aback at first, then he'd enthusiastically gotten with the program.

Rogan contemplated them, her, more intently. It wasn't jealousy—he was never jealous when Wes touched her—it was distrust. Not in her, but of her actions; like he couldn't believe she was suddenly over what had happened to her. She wasn't. But when it came down to it, no matter what he planned, she didn't want to die. She wanted to scream out *I don't want to die. I don't deserve this. I might have been bad, but not like this.*

When she was a child, that seed that had taken root, the one that told her she did deserve it. But she would do anything to combat that. Their leaving her behind would be a death sentence. She didn't want to be taken from them. So she would rally.

She climbed onto Wes and rode him under Rogan's assessing gaze. Eventually, he gave in. He lashed her to the headboard, and this time Wes was the spectator while Rogan manipulated her body to please himself. It was only a matter of time before they were simultaneously taking their pleasure from her.

If nothing else, she wanted to ensure they would miss this, they would miss her.

Because she would miss them.

33

FIRE

Rogan

Wes was right. He couldn't trust Narlina. There was no time to waste in putting a plan in place and executing it; they were one unstable woman's emotions away from catastrophe. For himself and Wes, it would be a death sentence. But his prize's sentence would make her wish for death.

From his seat at the table, he took her in. She was on her bed. He'd offered her the sofa, but she'd ignored him and curled up in the corner, her book in hand.

She'd been perfect. Better than he deserved. Her affection only increased his guilt. He owed her so much more than a place on the furniture. The obvious answer was to give back her voice, but he couldn't do that.

He'd become attached—a danger to them both now that Alan had noticed—even when he'd been striving for distance, attempting to guard against her. But he'd been fooling himself.

Hearing her voice now would break his concentration, undo him.

He *could* explain to her why. It wasn't as though she could challenge him on it. But as he watched her reading, he pussied out.

Get her off this island; that was what he could do for her. If they died trying, it would certainly be better than the fate that remained for her, for either of them, here.

Wes opened the door. "Help me out here."

Curious, Rogan went to the door, finding Wes with a large wooden box on the other side.

"Motherfucker's heavy."

Rogan leaned down and hefted one side. "What is this?"

Once inside the apartment, Wes shut the door and fell back against it. Blond hair darkened with sweat stuck to his forehead and neck. He let out an exaggerated breath and glanced at the woman in the corner. "Hey, baby doll."

Her eyes brightened at the endearment. A whisper of a smile tipped her lips up. Fuck, she was so fuckable. When she peered at him, she maintained her smile, but the brightness dimmed. He deserved it, her guarded response, but he returned the smile.

"It's an inflatable boat." Wes wiped the sweat away.

Rogan studied the crate. "It says *quilts* on the side."

"I couldn't have people watching me lug a boat around; they'd ask questions. No one gives a shit about blankets."

It was true. "How did you get—"

"Procurement, remember? That covers everything." They both looked over at the woman in the corner. The book was on her lap, and her attention was trained on them.

"And disposal." Wes tossed him a look, sharing in a moment of understanding of all that it entailed. "This is one of the damaged boats. It's been patched, though, so it should work."

"Should?"

"It's our best option, and no one will miss this, not for a while anyway." He reached into his back pocket and pulled out a metal instrument. "Now for the really unpleasant part."

At the sight of the scalpel, adrenaline charged through Rogan. He broke out in a light sweat. "This is happening tonight?" Was he ready? In theory, yes, but he'd thought he'd have more warning.

"No going back now, my friend. Everything is already in motion."

"Everything" meaning the distraction they'd planned to shift focus. Once it occurred, Rogan would send a code to the island's comms systems to take down the live feeds. Normally others would be working to bring it back online within minutes, but with two catastrophes at once, the cameras would hopefully not be a priority.

The scalpel Wes held would remove the tracking devices in their necks. The risks that accompanied this part were even more daunting, but they'd come too far for him to pussy out now, especially when there was a freaking boat in his living room.

Rogan nodded. "Prize!" he ordered.

Again, they both looked at her. Her eyes had gone wide, her skin paling.

Realizing her fear, he expanded, "Let's get that tracker out of you." He couldn't help but grin at her incredulous expression. "Unless you want to stay?"

She hesitated, looking unsure as to whether this was a game, as if she thought he and Wes would burst into laughter. He held his hand out to her, and that was enough. She lurched to her feet, beaming at him.

There. That was the expression he wanted from her.

• • • • • • • • •

Their girl squeaked when Wes cut into her neck, but she didn't wiggle or cry. Lying face down on the counter, she allowed the man to extract what he'd inserted months ago.

He slid the tiny device into a silicone holder, then placed a bandage on the incision to stop the blood. "Okay, you're…" He hesitated, clearing his throat. "Done."

Maybe Wes had wanted to say "free" but changed his mind. They weren't free, any of them, yet. And an RFID still resided beneath her skin, but it was useless unless she was scanned. No one scanned people on the mainland. At least, not for the purpose she was scanned here.

When she moved, Rogan took her place, leaning forward. The tracker could be removed; their tattoos were another matter. Once they were someplace safe, he and Wes would need to cover the tats with more ink, but he didn't want to jinx them by planning too far ahead.

Wes was last. Rogan raised his eyes to his prize before he made the initial incision. She was watching his hands, not him. There was a look he couldn't place on her face: doubt, maybe? Did she doubt them in their decision to include her and take her? Or was she doubting that this could work?

Maybe he was projecting. There were a lot of dominoes yet to fall into place before they made it off this island. Pausing in his task, he patted her cheek. "Any minute now, pet."

A loud bang sounded on the door. Wes snapped up straight. Rogan leaped back, almost vomiting; he knew that heavy-handed knock. Holy fuck. Although he knew it wasn't possible, the coincidence—the trackers being removed and a visitor showing up—was sickening.

Before any of them could move, the door swung open and Alan entered. Rogan flicked his attention over the man's shoulder, fully expecting him to be flanked by a group of men who would lead them away.

But Alan was alone.

Barely past the threshold, his attention was caught by the crate, a confused frown tugging at his lips. His accusing eyes flicked up to them. "Contraband?"

Rogan gently took his pet's arm, maneuvering her closer to him; she didn't need the encouragement. Her nails dug into his bicep as she slipped behind him.

"No," Wes answered. "Blankets."

Alan assessed the crate again, his demeanor full of suspicion. Rogan's stomach continued to twist. They'd been so fucking close. "Why is a crate of blankets in your apartment?"

"I was taking them to the east warehouse," Wes answered. "But they're heavy. I stopped to take a breather."

The older man's curiosity waned as he regarded the three in the kitchen. He scoffed. "A breather." By the sick twist of his lips, he was interpreting the scene in front of him differently. "Almost where I left you last time."

She was clutching his arm so hard her nails broke skin. He didn't flinch.

"Only now we have a third party to watch."

"Watch?" Rogan asked, blood whooshing in his ears.

"I told you I'd be back. And it appears as though you haven't learned your lesson."

No, he hadn't—wouldn't—learn these lessons. But Christ, why did this need to happen tonight?

"Wes can impress upon you the meaning of apathy. He's quite good at it, as he needs to be."

Beside Rogan, Wes was grinning like he'd been complimented. Paranoia raced through him. Disposal. Wes's tracker was still in place. The coincidence in timing was too fucking great.

When Wes looked his way, he winked. What the fuck did that mean?

Alan approached, snapping and pointing to the counter. "Put her there."

Her breaths were quiet and rapid against his back. He didn't move to bring her forward.

Wes piped up. "Wait, you're here for a fuck?"

"Yes. I'm teaching Rogan a lesson in dispassion." Snapping and pointing, he indicated the countertop again. "I want her ass. Now."

Wes rejoined cheerfully. "Well, hell, I've got an ass. I can do that." He unbuttoned and shoved his pants down, assuming the position meant for her. At the same time, he casually placed one hand over the encased trackers. Looking back over his shoulder at them, Wes grinned, smacking his own butt. "It's a pretty ass."

Relief flooded through him, followed by guilt that he'd suspected his friend.

Alan's face turned red. So red it bordered on purple. "I can ensure your ass is regularly fucked if you keep up these shenanigans, and you won't be grinning."

The smile faltered, but Wes shrugged as though unperturbed. "I like her ass the way it is. Take what's offered, old man. Perhaps I need a lesson, too."

"How *dare*—"

A blast rocked the foundation. Plates and glasses inside the cabinets rattled violently. His prize flattened herself against his back with a gasp. They all looked toward the front of the apartment; the blinds on the window were closed, but Alan had left the door open. The night sky was dancing with orange light.

Alarms rent the air, followed by shouting. People ran by the open portal, in the direction of the eerie orange glow. No one bothered to look inside the apartment. Disaster plans were immediately being implemented, which included the volunteer firefighters.

Wes straightened, pulling his pants back up, not bothering to look toward the commotion.

"What the *fuck*?" Alan screeched as he stormed toward the door. "You two, get to your positions."

Neither of them moved.

He halted at the door, glaring back at them. His attention swung back to the crate, his mind working, putting puzzle pieces into place. He reversed course and advanced on them. His voice was chilling. "You won't live long enough. And that bitch is mine."

Rogan body-blocked him. "No. She's mine."

Alan took a swing that Rogan dodged. Wes caught his fist. Rogan shoved his prize farther back. She tumbled to the ground, but he didn't stop to check on her. She was smart enough to steer clear.

"I'll see you both castrated and your dicks fed to you," Alan yelled, taking another swing at Wes, who blocked it. "And your little whore—"

"Rogan! Is it—Oh!"

Rogan's head snapped around toward the door.

Narlina stood there, her eyes wide. She wore black slacks and a black top. When she spotted her husband, her demeanor immediately morphed. "I knew it was you two!" She stormed inside and continued to yell. "I told you I knew you, Ro. I knew you were up to something."

"Why are you wearing those clothes? And why is your hair up?" The questions came from Alan.

Rogan knew why: they were clothes for hiding, for running. The silk dresses her husband dolled her up in wouldn't be practical. Her speed in getting to them after the building exploded was impressive; that she had the proper clothing, more so. As if she'd been prepared, waiting for this moment.

Despite the circumstances surrounding them, Rogan had to give her credit. She did know him.

Narlina's jaw dropped open, and her face drained of all color. She looked to Rogan for an answer—or for help getting her out of the predicament—but he slowly shook his head. She was on her own.

"Narlina! Answer me!" Alan's face was purple with fury and agitation. Literally everything was burning down around him, yet he was too preoccupied with maintaining control over three rebelling individuals to notice. Three, because to Alan, Rogan's pet wasn't considered a person.

Narlina stammered and ducked her chin, running her hands over the material as though how she became enshrouded in them was a mystery.

Wes let out a sarcastic huff. "You two are welcome to take your domestic troubles elsewhere. There's a fire on the island, in case you missed it."

As if punctuating his words, a series of pops rent the air; the sounds of a fire finding more fuel.

With a furious bellow, Alan spun and attacked Wes.

"No!" Narlina cried out, dashing forward. Rogan intercepted her and dragged her back. She screamed once before he slapped his hand over her mouth. He didn't know who she was yelling for, which angle she was playing, but the door was open. He didn't need her screams to draw attention.

Hopefully, the fire was enough distraction. The guests would either be watching the show or making a mad dash to the docks and helipad on the other side of the island to make their getaways. Their safe and anonymous departure during the chaos of a disaster had been well-orchestrated. The panic would be on the other side of the island, away from where they planned to launch from.

He hadn't known tonight was the night Wes would choose. Wes was spontaneous, though; he should have been prepared for anything at any time.

Nothing, however, could have prepared them for Alan's appearance. This was definitely not part of the plan.

34

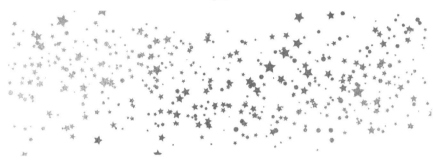

FIGHT
The Prize

No one ever fought for her. No one had ever stepped up to defend her, to help her, until this moment. No one had ever wanted to keep her. Her family had failed her. School counselors looked the other way or called her a liar. Friends, acquaintances, really, weren't genuine enough to care. Even Rogan had let her be brutally violated.

She'd never before *inspired* that kind of devotion; she'd been the one who fought for others, only to be abandoned when she had a need in return. But now, they were fighting for her. Rogan had chosen her. *Her.* Wes had offered his own body. It didn't erase the way he had chosen her originally and his past horrific methods, but he—they—were trying to right that wrong now.

That they were taking her with them was too difficult, too incredible, to internalize; she wanted to be excited. She wanted to feel *something* other than terror that this would be taken from her. It had happened many times before. She'd been given a gift so her joy could be bathed in. More satisfying to the giver was the act of taking away so her tears could be reveled in, her begging pleas giving them satisfaction, reinforcing their importance in her life. Give, take, give, take. Eventually, she learned not to show appreciation or excitement. Not for anything. Not about anything. Don't feel, don't react, feign indifference.

But she wanted this, the chance to run with them. This, she felt. She couldn't imagine being parted from them. So she would fucking fight for this, just as they were fighting for her.

The advantage of being a well-behaved, quiet little slave was that she wasn't perceived as a threat. With the exception of the day the men tried to take her from Rogan's home, she'd never fought back before, so why would she now? Because the man standing between her and freedom was also the man who'd raped her. Many men and women had, true, but this was the one who had taken what little shred of hope she'd had and was working to obliterate it.

She would not stay. So what was she willing to do?

Anything. The fighter in her might have been dormant, at the precipice of extinction, really, but it had been awakened. She would do fucking *anything* for them and for herself.

So the silent, good little pet, the doll, became an avenger, a fighter.

Her cloak of invisibility made it easy for her to go undetected as she slid open the kitchen drawer and took out the knife—one of the knives Wes and Rogan had joked about her using on them. No one noticed as she sidled along the kitchen island toward them, not even Rogan or Wes, as they struggled and fought. Fighting for her.

No, they were too preoccupied to watch this warrior rise.

Wes saw her one second before she struck. Her first blow came so quickly he didn't have time to react. Her knife embedded itself in the monster's neck, but not deep enough. It rebounded against bone, and the man let out a weird scream, his hand automatically flying to the wound. His face twisted in outrage and confusion as he turned toward her. In her peripheral vision, Wes's mouth was agape.

The second blow struck his throat. More true and intensely satisfying. A part of her soul was nourished in that moment by something she hadn't realized she'd been starved for. But it wasn't enough. The blood wasn't enough. His screams weren't enough. She raised her arm and brought it down once more. He staggered under her attack but didn't fall. She pulled her hand back and did it again. And again. Plunging and jabbing, even as the knife became slippery and sticky with his warm blood.

It might never be enough. Her broken heart on the boat, her time in the cages, her terror as she fell down the chute. These pitiful yells and cries weren't enough. *There wasn't enough blood.* The ravaged little girl stirred and thirsted for more, allowing this man to pay penance for so many others, and she was worth more than the offering he was giving. He brought his hands up to his neck, as if trying to stanch the gushing blood, and staggered back, colliding with the refrigerator.

She was distantly aware of other voices yelling—confusion and horror elsewhere—but her sole focus was on this man. She wanted her pound of flesh. No, she wanted his whole fucking body; she'd earned it.

His expression—his disbelief, anger, fear—filled her heart with satisfaction. She wanted to lick it off him, to savor the power she'd taken from him, the life she was stripping away. He'd always be a part of her. She may as well have his defeat, too.

She kept slashing. There was no way to count how many times she did so. Hands grasped her upper arms and pulled, but she rebelled. She would have her vengeance. She would take it for the others. He slid down the appliance, still attempting to keep in the pumping blood, and she followed him down.

If it was still pumping, he was still alive. That wasn't good enough.

"Doll!" The word permeated. It fed her. Fighting off the restraining hands, she sank to her knees with the shocked and pissed bastard. Her pain and fury and disgust poured into him as his blood poured out, decorating her and the floor. It felt like hours, but it was only seconds, before his eyes glazed over.

Dead.

Her heart felt like it had wings.

"Holy shit, Doll!"

The voice was filled with awed laughter. She allowed him to drag her away. He pulled her to her feet as she slid in the warm, sticky liquid. His hand was over hers, taking the knife. She let him have it as she stared silently at her dead tormentor. She was suddenly very tired, but this wasn't the time for a nap.

The other noises in the room seeped in. She didn't have to look to know that Rogan was restraining Narlina; she heard the stifled screams.

But she turned to them anyway.

"Shut the fuck up!" Rogan ordered, his hand over her mouth.

When Narlina noticed her attention, she stilled, her eyes going wide with fear.

But she didn't have an issue with Narlina. No, the only issue between them was Narlina's hatred of her. Her jealousy.

Jealous. Her heart soared even higher. The beautiful woman was jealous of the devotion a slave had earned. A giggle threatened to escape her, but she tamped it down. The time for celebration would come later.

"Fuck me. You're full of surprises."

Her attention shifted to Wes.

Beside her, his eyes were wary, but his shoulders were pulled back, almost as if he were proud. Mostly, though, he looked freaked out. Because of her? Or because she hadn't done the same thing to him?

Narlina wriggled and yelled behind Rogan's hand again.

She raised an eyebrow as the woman struggled. If Wes hadn't taken the knife, she might have been convinced to dispatch her just to shut her up. But she was unarmed—albeit surrounded by drawers of tools—so she watched.

"C'mon, Doll. Help me with the boat."

She ignored Wes, wondering what Rogan would do with Narlina.

"We'll have to take her with us," Rogan said over Narlina's head.

Pained fury raced through her. Take her with them? No, that's not how this was supposed to work. She stood taller, her expression angry.

Wes took her arm and pulled her toward the crate. "You might want to rethink that plan; this one is on a hair-trigger." He jerked his head in her direction as he lifted the lid, exposing what looked like a pile of black rubber.

The amusement in his tone held a touch of uncertainty. She assessed Rogan. Why didn't he do to his former love what he'd done to her almost every time he'd left and shackle her to the bed? Was it because the thought of doing so was unconscionable when it came to Narlina? It was good enough for a pet, but not for… what? A woman he saw as human?

"Just fucking gag her and tie her up, man. We don't have the time for it. And she won't fit; there's a weight limit."

She smiled at Wes in approval.

He gave her a wary double take as he straightened. "My gorgeous girl, you look downright terrifying right now."

She appreciated the *gorgeous* comment, but she couldn't help but wonder if he'd said it to keep her from losing her shit again. She wouldn't. The problem had been handled. But she probably did look scary, decorated in blood and smiling. The mental image made her smile broaden.

Rogan took the suggestion and dragged Narlina down the hall. There was a short scream, probably when Rogan removed his hand, but it was cut off quickly, likely by a gag. Moments later, he rejoined them, tapping out something on his phone.

Looking up, he caught her frown of disapproval. "Setting everything else in motion, pet."

She liked their uncertainty. But she loved that despite what she assumed was their uncertainty of her sanity, they were still taking her.

Tight-lipped, Rogan assisted with the boat; it was deceptively heavy.

Was he really okay with leaving Narlina behind? Or was his dark expression one of regret over the situation?

He caught her look as they shuffled toward the door. As though reading her mind, he shook his head. Then he assessed her. She was wearing his bloodied t-shirt and nothing else.

"Hold on." Rogan disappeared back down the hallway.

She stared after him, her heart pounding in trepidation, suddenly certain that he'd reappear with Narlina. Relief washed over her when he came back with clean clothes, including leggings, for her.

He held them out. "Change."

She eagerly took the clothes and stripped quickly. She tossed the bloodied shirt into the empty crate.

Wes jerked his chin toward the wooden box. "That gives me an idea. It might buy us time."

She stood back as Rogan and Wes dragged the crate into the kitchen, then lifted the dead man and tossed him in. Rogan looked skeptical; she understood his skepticism, because though they'd hidden the body, there was still blood everywhere.

"It's a little less obvious," Wes said. He and Rogan contemplated their handiwork for only a minute before they simultaneously turned their attention to her. She tried not to look as proud of herself as she felt, but she must have failed, because Wes shook his head and grinned at her.

As best as they could with the contraption, they raced toward the water's edge. It was hard to see in the moonless night. Though the fire was still blazing, it was far enough away that the light from it did not reach them. Darkness encased them, and the matte black boat would be unseen in the inky water.

In the background, another type of alarm clanged. Either the fire was getting bigger or the island was being evacuated. Or the dead man had been found, and therefore Narlina.

They waded out far enough to keep from drifting back in. Wes grabbed her and tossed her into the boat, then assisted Rogan in. They turned and offered their hands to him.

Wes shook his head, pushing the boat farther out. "I'm not going with you."

Her heart stopped.

Rogan demanded what she didn't. "What? What the fuck are you talking about? Get in the boat!"

"It won't work this way."

He was leaving her? No, he couldn't do it. She reached for him, panicking. Her pants were erratic as she tried to grasp on to him.

"Buying time." Wes fought her desperately grabbing hands. "I'm sorry. I never should have brought you here, but I'm going to make damn sure you get away, that you're safe."

A wail worked its way up her throat, and tears filled her eyes. Determined, she leaned over to grab him, to force him into the boat with them.

He took advantage of her position and grasped her behind her neck. She didn't even feel the cut there as he pulled her to him.

"I love the fuck out of you, baby doll." He crashed his mouth into hers, feeding her the love he'd once given her, the love she'd lost on another boat, seemingly ages ago.

She was as stunned by his actions as his words, but more, she was devastated. She couldn't let him do this. She couldn't let him go. He took hold of her wrists and pushed her away.

He addressed Rogan. "Get her out of here and take care of her."

She struggled, half-rising to leave the boat.

Rogan wrapped his arm around her waist, pulling her back despite her resistance. "We have time, Wes. Get in the fucking boat. There are distractions everywhere. You don't need to be another."

Rogan sounded as panicked as she felt.

Wes shook his head. "They'll figure it out and follow. If Narlina has been found, she's talking." He shoved the boat hard before stepping away, avoiding her hands. He fought the water as he continued backward, his arms out to balance himself. He continued his stumbling pace backward, calling out, "She's worth the sacrifice."

"Wes. It's a death sentence."

Ignoring Rogan's words, he grinned at her and pointed. "Be a good girl. Miss me."

She did. She did, so much, already. But she didn't want to miss him; she wanted him here with her. She didn't take her eyes from him as the boat glided farther out, just as his didn't leave her as he continued to back away, moving closer to the shore. Rogan's restraining arm was tight around her. With his free hand, he started the motor. With the sounds of the ocean overpowering it, it was practically silent.

Their little boat shot forward, away from Wes.

Her heart; holy fuck, her heart. She couldn't leave him. They couldn't leave *them*. They were a trio. He was a horrible person, but he was her horrible person as much as she was his. She struggled more urgently in Rogan's hold, squeals of anguish escaping her.

Wes was getting smaller, his body a dark shadow. The only thing distinguishable now was his lighter hair.

They made good time across the calmer waters. Soon enough, they would head into the larger waves. Even when Wes was indistinguishable, she wouldn't look away.

The shadow moved suddenly, running.

Her gasp of horror drew Rogan's attention.

What echoed across the water sounded like a gunshot. She lurched forward, a scream on her lips. As Wes's name was ripped from her throat, Rogan grabbed her back and slapped a hand over her mouth. He wrestled her to the bottom of their boat.

He didn't offer words of reassurance; there were none to be had. His heavy breathing told her everything she needed to know: he was hurting, too. Hurting because Wes was dead. She sobbed against his hand, grieving the man who loved her. Her tormentor but also the one who'd shielded her. Protected her. Saved her.

Did she deserve his sacrifice?

35

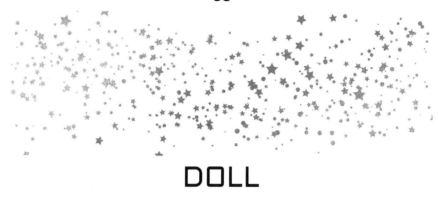

DOLL

Rogan

Her screams against his palm eventually quieted. Her struggles waned. Her hot tears dripping over his hand subsided. Either she sensed or realized they were too far away to go back and help what was most likely a dead man, or her grief had finally overpowered her. Once he was certain that she'd calmed, he carefully released her, though he watched her closely in case she jumped out of the boat. He hadn't expected a single one of her reactions tonight.

He returned to the motor and redirected the small boat. Ahead, tiny lights were barely visible, twinkling in and out of sight as they were tossed on the waves. The mainland. It was so close, yet an entire life away.

They weren't safe, not by a longshot. He could only pray that they made it to shore before a larger, faster boat came after them. He looked at her where she'd moved to huddle at his feet. Even in the inky darkness, he could see her face twisted in anguish. She was turned in the direction of the island, the glitter of her tears sparkling in the moonless night.

He'd made a promise to Wes to keep her; keep her safe. He would. She was his. She was theirs. He'd keep that promise. Wes had admitted that he never should have brought her to the island. There was truth in that. She hadn't belonged there—no one did. And Rogan had hated her, his golden prize whose existence mocked his own captivity.

But he wouldn't have left without her, couldn't have. If anyone else had tumbled at his feet, he wouldn't have risked all for them. Wes wouldn't have, either.

He stroked her spray-dampened hair. His silent prize was his pet no longer. She was now as free as he was, no matter how long that freedom lasted. He didn't want to wait to make it to the mainland; he would give everything back to her now. "What's your name?"

Eyes still swimming with grief, she considered him, but she didn't answer. Had she forgotten? Had she resigned herself so intently to being his prize that she wouldn't speak, or didn't know how to answer?

"What's your *real* name?"

Over her head, the city lights danced, teasing, bobbing up and down in time to the boat cutting through the rough water. Closer. They were closer. He turned his full attention to her, to their forward momentum. The urge to look back, like she was doing, was strong, but ahead of him lay everything: the city, a new beginning, her.

It was time she reclaimed all that had been ripped from her. "Miss, what's your name?" Like they were strangers, meeting for the first time. In a sense, they were.

Finally, she replied in her sexy, raspy voice. "Dahlia."

He beheld her, studied her. For a few minutes, he couldn't speak. His throat had closed up with emotion. "Dahlia," he repeated shakily. Tears leapt to his eyes, the realization devastating him. She might have been his prize, but Wes hadn't stripped her of everything. "*Doll.*"

36

FREEZE

Rogan

With her hand gripped firmly in his, Rogan led her across the crowded beach toward the bright lights and loud music, toward a world she knew, a world that was foreign to him. This was not unlike that first walk they'd taken along the beach, where he'd had her stumbling after him.

The dread was too powerful. The fear that the lights were illuminating them for predatory and vengeful eyes made it impossible to feel even an ounce of relief. So he led her away from the threats, toward the shelter of the buildings. By the dazed expression she'd worn when he lifted her from the boat, he surmised that, for now, he had to lead her.

He moved with confident, determined strides. He wanted to appear comfortable in his skin and trajectory to anyone who noticed them. No one looked, though. They were anonymous, invisible in the crowd, but he was still paranoid. It was more for her sake than his. He'd failed her once—more than once—he would not fail both her and Wes.

Her trust in him, her acquiescence, humbled him. She was free. She was again part of a society she understood and could manipulate. At any moment, she could scream and run from him, pointing an accusing finger. He would have no defense against her. He would succumb to her wishes, her desires, her blame; he wouldn't want to be parted from her, unable to care for her and fulfill his pledge to Wes, but if she was hurt by his presence, he would go.

His heart lurched painfully, anticipating the moment her shock wore off and she tore herself from him. It wouldn't matter then that he'd had to physically pluck her from the now-abandoned contraption because she hadn't been able to bring herself to voluntarily leave it, as if staying in it would freeze time, would maintain a connection to Wes.

Was Wes dead? There would be no way to find out. His friend was cunning and knew how to play most things to his advantage. He'd take solace in that.

Rogan had doubted his loyalty on more than one occasion—had done so this very night. But there was no way to explain a dead man, especially with Narlina as witness. *Their* disappearance, Rogan imagined, could be explained. Because an explanation would be demanded. Alan was gone, but Larry and Trent were there. As prepared as they were for any disaster, certainly they had directives in the event that something happened to Alan.

The memory of the gunshot sent a chill through him. He'd seen Wes running. He'd heard the burst as clearly as Dahlia had. It could have been many things, couldn't it? But for as much as he wanted his friend to be alive, a quick death would have been merciful.

Yeah, Wes could talk himself out of most anything. But Narlina was a wildcard. He should have killed her, but that was one act he couldn't bring himself to do. Not to her, his childhood friend, his onetime lover. In a way, she was as innocent as Dahlia. Killing her might have been a mercy, but it wasn't one he was capable of providing her. But had leaving one friend alive resulted in the death of another?

A hiccupping sound caught his attention above the din of people, vendors, and loud music. Maybe it was because he had been waiting for this moment, for her to break. Turning abruptly, he absorbed the force of the impact when she barreled into him, caught off guard by his about-face. Releasing her hand, he pulled her to him with one arm, his other hand cradling her head against his chest.

His heart was in his throat. Would she fight, scream, rebel against him?

She didn't. Instead, she collapsed against his chest, wrapping her arms around his waist. She was shaking. Hot tears soaked his damp shirt. Her small catches of breath turned into sobs. This was grief. Shock. Maybe even a little relief. But she was clinging to him like he was her lifeline. The sounds escaping her were those of her soul being ravaged and simultaneously liberated.

His own vision was blurred by tears as he cradled her, comforted her, grieved with her. He attempted to soothe, whispering platitudes in her ear.

"Y'all okay?" a man shouted.

Rogan looked up, and Dahlia tensed in his arms. His own heart had leapt into his throat, and panic gripped him for a moment. In that flash, he was certain that they'd been chased and found. But it was another couple, the man squinting in curiosity. The woman beside him was more openly suspicious and accusing.

"We're okay," Rogan answered. "She's upset."

She shifted to look up at him.

He gently wiped a tear from her cheek with his thumb.

"Are you sure?" the woman insisted. "You can come with us."

Panic raced through him for another reason. He kept his gaze on her, though, scared of her answer. But he asked anyway. "This is your chance—your choice—my pretty little prize. What do you want?"

She gave him a wary look filled with uncertainty and fear, like he was mocking her.

Cupping her cheek, he pressed his forehead to hers. "I don't want you to choose to leave me, but if you do, I'll let you go. But before you decide, you need to know that if you stay, I'll be devoted to you. I'm yours, more than you were ever mine."

Her scrutiny was intense, even a touch accusing. He couldn't say how long they stood there as he waited for her decision, his heartbeat banging in his ears. He no longer heard the humanity surrounding them or the distant waves. He no longer cared about the expectant couple. She was his world, all he breathed in, all he saw. He would have stood there all night for her.

When she moved, it was to step back, her chin kicking up defiantly. She took his hand while simultaneously tossing the waiting couple a smile. Shaking her head at them, refusing their assistance, she led him away. Before long, they mingled with the masses, her actions firmly entrenching her in his heart. He'd follow her anywhere.

His prize, his gift. Her.

37

FLIGHT
The Prize

She'd once heard that only one percent of trafficked individuals make it out. By those odds, escape from a place like that shouldn't have been possible. She and Rogan had gotten away thanks to Wes. He'd done it for her, for them. He'd gone back to buy her and Rogan time. In essence, he'd died for them. It was the weightiest of realities. He had loved her. With that final act, it was easy to acknowledge that truth. She'd been loved by him. If only she had been in a place to hear him—literally and figuratively—when he'd said it. But it had been impossible for her to accept such words under those circumstances.

The voice in the back of her head taunted that she shouldn't accept the sentiments even now. That she didn't deserve them. She'd never be free from that voice, that doubt, despite Rogan's reminders and assurance. Somewhere in her twenty-some years, she'd resigned herself to the understanding that she'd never experience an anxiety-free moment, would never understand what it meant to be easy with love; her brain was damaged forever.

Rogan had deferred to her to choose their final destination. She hadn't wanted to leave the city, even if they were so poor they had to sleep on the streets. She'd felt closer to Wes there. Rogan assured her that he'd left a message for Wes in their common spot in the city. If Wes managed to survive and make it off the island, he could find them. Neither said the words out loud, but both understood that it was more likely that he didn't survive. They'd been in Puerto Rico for two years and had given up hope. Not that they'd had much to begin with.

Considering she'd escaped a sex slave operation, and had killed a man, reclaiming her identity hadn't been practical. Besides, they were miles and miles from her home. And there was always the "if." If they were on someone's agenda, if that person were to hunt them down, it would be best to avoid that connection. It wasn't worth the risk at the time. Not until later did she decide a survivor of that situation wouldn't be tracked down; she had no value to them and, unfortunately, was easily replaceable. Any hunting for her would be because of Alan's demise, but not because they'd lost a whore.

Besides, the woman she'd been then wasn't who she was now. And after an Internet search of her name, her heart ached even more severely. Because no one had looked. No one had missed her. So returning to a life where no one cared or wanted her didn't make sense. She hadn't used her name since that night on the inflatable boat. After all, it was wrapped up in torture, torment, and hurt. Dahlia was the name of a victim, and she wasn't a victim anymore; she was a survivor.

Wes's motivations, she'd never have answers for. She didn't understand his motives for kidnapping her, despite what he'd told her, despite what he'd done for her in the end. He'd put her through so much, only to sacrifice himself to ensure her safety. Sure, if he hadn't, they likely would have been found immediately and returned. Then what would have happened to her? Death, she assumed, though there were punishments worse than death.

Following the tenants of hiding in plain sight, they remained in the Caribbean. Their safe haven was an unassuming one-room home in the southern part of the island, a place they'd had to earn. They'd worked their way up to renting in cash after sleeping in various odd spots for months. They lived off the grid as much as they could. Their neighbors in the *barrio* grew to accept them. Her mastery of Spanish helped ease the way. Rogan had been stunned when she'd started conversing. Then he'd grinned with pride. Maybe some relief, too.

His smile was rare—though not as rare as her own—but they were discovering joy in the little things. And each other. Finding their footing with one another had taken a while, as though they were two strangers thrown together; in a sense, they were. They were re-examining their roles.

Rogan had been to the mainland many times, but she knew how to move easily through society, even if she didn't want to. For many things, he deferred to her. He'd never known she was bilingual or that she had been working toward a degree in hospitality management with a minor in culinary arts. He took in all of this knowledge while wearing conflicting expressions, both impressed and sorrowful. The sadness, she guessed, wasn't for her alone, but for the nameless people he'd had a hand in victimizing. Those like her, with lives and aspirations that had been stolen from them.

She taught him Spanish, and about holidays. He was familiar with them, though holidays weren't celebrated on the island, with the exception of Christmas—even if the origin story was lost on him; there was no Christ where he'd come from. They had that in common. There was no Christ where she'd come from, either, but there had been gifts.

He'd penetrated her with an intense stare before stating passionately, "You're all I need."

Why did she stay with him? Other than for the moments when he said words like that? She knew what trauma bonds were; she was educated and aware enough to understand that, on some level, that's all it was between them. But it felt like more. He'd chosen her. And now he cared for her. She didn't want to jinx it and assign a strong emotion to it, because each time she had in the past, it had backfired. But she wanted to be with him; she wanted to see his smile on the rare occasion it peeked out. She wanted his hands and mouth on her. She wanted his cock inside her. She melted when he put his arm around her as they walked through the weekend farmers' market. She valued the little things he did for her, like bringing coffee to her in bed and hunting for the coqui at dusk with her, although the sticky little suckers found their way into the house.

Despite refusing to name the feeling outright, it lived inside her. It was a scary thing to admit, considering the last man she loved. The one who had presumably died for her. But Rogan had fought for her; both men had. That was loyalty; that was something like love. It was a new sensation, but it was real; after all, there was a man no longer breathing because he'd threatened Rogan and Wes. Of course, his greater sin was abusing her and dismissing her. His sins would take her a lifetime to recount, and she'd only seen him three times.

To this day, she seldom spoke. Rogan urged her to talk to him or sing with him when he turned on their little radio. He'd attempt to dance, looking silly, trying to draw her out. He'd wear a look of guilt and apology when she'd maintain her silence, even if she did join him in dancing. She didn't do it to make him feel guilty. Being silent had been a comfort, and *she* decided now when she spoke, not Rogan. It was freeing, and when she did say something, it made her words that much more valuable. He'd hang on them, thirsty for more, but her voice was for herself.

Another was her need—and it was a need—for a collar. Not a dog collar, like he'd once put on her, but a choker. It comforted her to wear it; she'd asked him to pick it out from a selection made by a local craftsman. He'd gaped at her for a minute, as if trying to get a read on her and the request. Then his eyes had flared with possessiveness. He picked out a silver-painted one wide enough for two snaps.

As she reclaimed her independence, their sex became even hotter. They only had each other now, and it wasn't unusual for desperation and fear to haunt their passion as they missed their messy partner. During sex, she was vocal, crying out, moaning, her strangled shrieks causing him to clap his hand over her mouth so the neighbors didn't hear.

Sometimes they made love tenderly, a never-ending adventure in discovering what pleased the other; more frequently, it was fast and furious, as if they were trying to outrun the ghosts that chased them.

Nightmares claimed them both; they'd taken turns holding one another, offering comfort. They never promised that it would be okay, because it wasn't. It wouldn't be. Nothing that had happened had been okay; they wouldn't lie to one another about that.

Her sleep was disturbed by memories of all that had happened and her powerlessness over her circumstances. While she had been enduring, her mind hadn't allowed her to fully process and succumb to the horror, much like when she was a child. Her subconscious's goal had been to survive first, then find a safe place to fall apart. Ironically, that safe place was in Rogan's arms. Only in her dreams did she revisit the night she was taken, her childhood, and how lessons learned had saved her life.

What she'd done to Alan never once disturbed her sleep. They never talked about it, the two of them, that which she was capable of: murder. Only, she didn't look at it that way. There had been an obstacle to her freedom, a threat, and her heart had demanded vengeance. Pushed to a certain point, she was certain everyone had that in them. They just didn't look the truth in the face, or they were lucky enough not to have to toe that line. She had, and she had no regrets. No regrets over killing the man who had raped her. Though she had other pangs of conscience—namely Wes.

She'd been riddled with guilt regarding her obligation to the innocents left behind. The men, women, and children that had also been taken.

Rogan had sent encrypted files to an FBI website from the Bahamas. He'd used a location remote enough not to have cameras but advanced enough to have the Internet. They'd watched the news in a local bar, waiting for something to happen—an exposé similar to another infamous island.

Days, weeks, and months passed. Nothing happened. It devastated her. Would she like to think she was a hero, rampaging to save lives? Of course. But she wasn't. Taking on the sex slave industry when she was no one, with one man supporting her, wasn't realistic. The devastating truth was that even if she had, she wouldn't have prevailed in that fight. She'd barely made it out. Those people were lost to the world, just like Dahlia Foster. More people would be lost tomorrow. Her helplessness at moments was so crushing she couldn't move.

Rogan motivated her by reminding her that they needed to pay rent, that she had survived, and that they needed to keep surviving. He'd rock her in his arms, telling her that justice was slow, placating her, assuring her that one day it would come. She knew it wouldn't. But her heart appreciated him even more for all his efforts to keep her from succumbing to her demons.

Rogan worked odd jobs, from construction to the pineapple fields to janitorial tasks at events. She used her skills to find a job as a cook in a local restaurant not often frequented by tourists. Learning how to prepare the local cuisine fed her soul.

At the moment, she was making a jibarito, absently listening to the chatter of her coworker, a few other local customers, and a tourist. She knew it was a tourist because the newcomer spoke English. Her friends enjoyed using their language skills with these rare passersby.

The locals had asked the man how he'd heard about this place and where he'd been on the island so far. He'd told them that finding this place had been a happy coincidence. Said he'd been in the mountains and chuckled about the narrow roads. Was grateful to be on lower ground.

They asked about his scars. Had he been in a fire? He had. A warehouse fire that spread. His burns were from his attempt to pull a woman from a burning apartment; he didn't succeed. She'd died.

His answer generated more questions. The raspy-voiced man patiently answered, his responses almost whispers; some, she couldn't hear over the frying of the plantain. Her heart had panged at the few times he chortled in response to questions. It was a familiar sound from a stranger.

After plating the sandwich and plantain chips, she walked out of the kitchen. Since he'd arrived, her co-worker had been urging her to make a rare appearance.

He was perched at the wooden bar near the open window of the kitchen. His straw hat obscured his face, and his head was turned as he took in the spectacular view of the Caribbean Sea.

She studied what she could see of him as she approached with the food, tilting her head in order to peek under his cap. The side of his face was covered with scars, as was what she could see of his arms. Her immediate response was empathy. It looked painful. When he turned toward her, she dropped the plate. It broke at her feet. The shattering was reversed in her heart. In that instant, it was whole for the first time in maybe her entire life. As ravaged as his face was, she'd know those blue eyes anywhere.

"Hey, Doll. Miss me?"

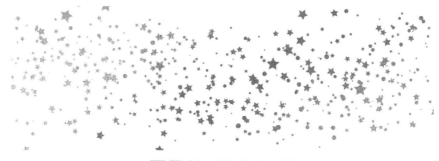

EPILOGUE

Wes

Would they make it, the three of them? The question played on a loop while he lay in bed with her sleeping between them. Each night, the uncertainties crept in. Did she love him? Could she? He'd been the instigator of her nightmares. He now *looked* like a nightmare. It didn't matter that she'd never blinked at his scars, that when he touched her, she melted, that she gave him shy smiles, uncertainty in her own eyes, like she was afraid *he* couldn't love *her*. Impossible; he'd always love her. He was the one who had started all of this, after all. He'd needed her so much that he'd had to have her with him.

During the quiet moments, though, the doubts became louder.

They'd beaten the odds before, all three of them, in different ways. She'd been trafficked *by him*, they'd escaped, he was scarred, and they were all silently wearing the badges of murderers. This last truth probably should have bothered them all, but it didn't. The deaths were necessary to protect her. To avenge her. He'd walk into a fiery hell over and over to ensure her safety, and Rogan was part of that.

The more time they spent away from the island of their captivity, the more he and Rogan began to understand the full horror of their own experiences. Their moments of devolving and deconstructing were the ones he knew she felt most useful to them. She'd had a lifetime steeped in trauma, after all, a childhood she'd had to survive. And she had, just as she'd survived Wes, Rogan, and the island. Now, she shared with them her tortured and twisted tools. So, in the end, they needed her as much as she needed them.

Was it fucked up? Yes. Did she lash out at them, panicked that they would leave her? Far too often. But they fought for her as much as she fought against them. It was a toxic cycle, but it worked. The love was real. For him, it had been so real that he'd been compelled to drag her into his world. It was dark and ugly, their love, but what else could it be, born in such a place and under those circumstances? The ugliness made it more real, more raw. They trusted it more because of the darkness of it, not despite it.

"Doll."

She had a new name, one he'd tattooed on his wrist. His brand resembled her own. Rogan had done the same. It was a further declaration of their commitment to her. Despite choosing a name of her own, she preferred the names they'd given her.

Heeding his summons, she rolled onto her side and met his gaze. She simultaneously snuggled back against Rogan, wriggling her bottom against his crotch. The heat flaring in his friend's eyes in response to her suggestive and enticing movements was no doubt accompanied by the hardening of his dick.

Rogan groaned, placing his hand on her hip to pull her more tightly against him. "Pet."

She smirked.

Wes loved her confidence; loved it even more when she caressed his chest and slid her hand toward his stiff cock, her lust and love reflecting back at him. In these moments, he believed both men were beautiful to her. Rogan had chosen her. Wes bore the scars of his devotion.

She was their doll, their pet, their prize. She belonged to them, with them.

Yes, they would make it.

Afterword

I've heard it said many times that everyone has one novel in them. Although I've written since I was a child, I've never considered my stories to be anything other than my outlet. I started a different version of this years ago because I needed to be heard even if the computer was the only audience. *One Novel* was the title, and it wasn't fiction. However, some realities are more easily digested when the audience is given the ability to distance themselves, when they're given the ability to not think about what may or may not be true, to suspend disbelief. I will leave that to the reader.

Prize's experiences are based in reality—actual events that occurred—but they are wrapped in fiction. I needed a voice; she is mine. I appreciate the irony of her being silenced while she screams truths.

The title chapters for our Prize's POV are intentional. Look at them again and you will see that the terms are related to cPTSD, with the exception of one or two.

Am I worried someone might recognize him or herself in this story? No. If so, I can't imagine anyone stepping up and claiming to be the party responsible for the things in this story. Also, names are changed or altered, and many others are not given names. Even if someone recognizes him or herself within, there is nothing to identify them by. But maybe the realization will prompt some self-reflection (although I doubt it). I know who they are and that's what matters.

Apropos of the topic, please see below for a few resources in the US:

National Human Trafficking Hotline: 888-373-7888 https://humantraffickinghotline.org

National Sexual Assault Hotline: 800-656-2673 https://rainn.org/

Childhelp National Child Abuse Hotline: 800-4-A-CHILD (800-422-4453) https://www.childhelp.org

cPTSD Foundation: https://cptsdfoundation.org/

I tried very hard not to glorify trafficking. The toxic, dysfunctional love found in this story is not meant to romanticize that which too many suffer. A few sources I consulted are below:

Allan, C., Winters, G. M., & Jeglic, E. L. (2023, May). *Current trends in Sex Trafficking Research*. Current psychiatry reports. https://www.ncbi.nlm.nih.gov/pmc/articles/PMC10113716/

Krell, M. (2022). *Taking down Backpage: Fighting the world's largest sex trafficker*. (S. Sheckells, Narr.) [Audiobook]. Tantor. New York University Press.

Nichols, A. J. (2016). *Sex trafficking in the United States: Theory, research, policy, and Practice*. Columbia University Press.

Stopping Traffic Productions. (2021). *Surviving Sex Trafficking*. Retrieved from http://survivingsextraffickingfilm.com

Acknowledgments

This story wasn't easy to write, and it barely toes the edge of romance, although it has *my* kind of happy ending. It is definitely dark. I honestly don't have the capacity to gauge its impact—big or small or at all—on any reader. So I need to thank my dedicated and brave betas for volunteering their time to read an initial, unedited, raw version of this tale (some offering and completing a second beta read!):

1. Longtime supporter and friend, Shilo Artis. I am so happy you like my stories! Earning your stamp of approval has been an honor!

2. Fellow writer and enthusiastically dedicated reader with a keen eye, Jess Elizabeth. You have no idea how much your support has meant. I'm looking forward to the day when I can reciprocate (although my vids won't be nearly as flawless or amazing as yours.)

3. Incredibly thorough, thoughtful, and supportive Author Cathryn Carter. I will never forget your sweet response of "I watch them" on my TikTok years ago when I said no one watches. I'm doubly happy because I love your stories! Cathryn is the one who suggested adding a Prologue.

4. Always supportive Crystal Fisk—thank you, also, for consistently

liking/sharing my posts and boosting. You are tireless and I appreciate it all so much!

5. Honest and detailed Shellina (@shellreada). I hope you approve of the rewrite. ;-)

6. Dolores Neumiller, a valued reader-turned-supporter. Your enthusiasm to read everything I write hits; thank you so much!

7. The beta readers preferring to remain anonymous: you know I heart you hard.

Thank you, thank you, thank you all! Your collective feedback enabled me to enhance this story for everyone.

I really wanted to get this one right, so after I made the initial changes, I sent this to a trusted source, J-V Jones, for the male perspective. I love your comment (and surprise, lol) that I write like I *have* a dick. Highest praise, BFAM!

Jeanine Harrell, indieeditswithjeanine.com, provided the developmental review. You can thank her for pushing me to restructure a bit, which gave you all Wes's point of view.

Beth Lawton has edited all of my manuscripts. She provided line, content, and proofreading for this story, and I am so grateful for her attention to detail and professionalism, although I almost fainted at how many redlines this one had. Gah, thank you so much for struggling through it and perfecting it for me. (And I still don't know what "what does that look like?" looks like, haha). You can find Beth at vbeditsromance.com

Kevin. Dude. You deserve a gold medal and hazard pay for constantly pulling me back from the brink. Since 2020, you've been busy, esp. when my manuscripts were stolen. And most recently when my trip down the trauma tunnel was orchestrated by someone I thought was a friend. Thank you for the homework assignments instructing me not to erase myself when that *continues* to be a solid option. I mean, sometimes I think more along the lines of "freaking asshole" for it, but (1) you read that with the humor intended, and (2) I mean it (the thanks). You have to admit this story is a far more entertaining reference source into my fucked-up brain than your notes.

A special shout out to Freya Victoria (narrator and author). The writing of this story has been languishing for years. I appreciate your encouragement to finish it. Well, here it is. "Ta-*daaaah*!"

Last, but certainly not least, to my wee group of faithful readers who take a chance on everything I write and love my people as much as I do. This one is a departure, for sure, so THANK YOU to those who have already read it and loved it. For those picking it up for the first time: THANK YOU for taking a chance on it. I hope you like it.

Also by Lilly...

THOSE WHO ARE BOUND

Being restrained isn't what anyone wants. Not emotionally, anyway. But Elliott is:

Shackled by guilt.

Ensnared by grief.

Tethered by dark, taboo secrets.

Immured by wicked desires.

After learning about Jonah's responsibilities, she becomes convinced that he is:

Caged by expectation.

Constrained by belief.

But Jonah is the only man who has been able to rid her of the emotional ropes she's wrapped herself up in.

Jonah has the uncanny understanding that Elliott is freed when caged. But he's the one man she's desperate to save from herself.

All Jonah wants to do is bind her to him.

Content warnings include suicide, mature situations, non-consent, violation of religious symbols, references to SA including SA of a minor.

THE TURBULENCE SERIES
ENTANGLEMENT (PART ONE)

Brit Delany found some semblance of peace by ignoring the pain of her past.

An American photojournalist working on the international stage, it was easy to distance herself from her traumatic childhood. But she is now heading back to Ireland, home of those turbulent memories.

Thankfully, there are friendly faces waiting for her. Two men, though last she saw them, they were the kindhearted boys who shepherded her through the worst of her dark and tumultuous days. Both look forward to her homecoming, but for far different reasons.

Secrets await in the Emerald Isle, and they will threaten everything Brit thought she knew. Love. Rejection. Obsession. Betrayal. All she's survived will act as her emotional armor for what is to come.

Entanglement ends with a cliffhanger. Tranquility is the conclusion to Entanglement.

TRANQUILITY (PART TWO)

When love becomes an obsession, when love betrays; when a man's love leads to unspeakable sins.

When love becomes a possibility, when love shelters; when a man's love leads to frightening revelations.

Brit Delany struggles to emerge from the darkness after surviving a chilling ordeal. She is forced to come to grips with the secrets of her past. But how does she learn to trust herself? How does she trust anyone around her? How does she find the strength to accept one man's love while reeling from the destructive passion of another?

How does she prevent her deepest fears from derailing everything and keeping her from the man she wants? Because in Brit's world, love always betrays.

Tranquility is the conclusion of Entanglement. Lilly's stories are not intended/appropriate for readers under 18 years of age. Be forewarned that the Turbulence Series addresses a range of traumatic issues, including child abuse and sexual assault.

HOLDING ON TO DAY

A second chance? Why would Cassidy want one? She's already had everything she could possibly want: a husband, a baby on the way, the perfect life... until it all crumbled away. Now, two years after her husband's death, Cassidy is barely holding on. Her interests don't go beyond her quiet existence on the lake or her German shepherd, Fred. ...That is, until an arrogant jerk buys the place next door and steals her dog.

A second chance? Mac doesn't need one. Or anyway, he doesn't deserve one. Mac bought a dilapidated cabin because it mirrors his state of mind: broken, isolated, useless to humanity. Plus, the place is close enough to town that he can drink himself into oblivion. He has no interest in connections except for one-night stands and commandeered time with his neighbor's dog. That is, unless you count Cassidy.

It's a second chance: the one they both need.

At first, Cassidy and Mac merely exist next to each other, but the attraction between them—the bond of their broken existence—pulls them together again and again. They aren't always the best people, but the jagged edges of their lives begin to heal each other, even as they strike out against it.

EVIE: A TURBULENCE SERIES NOVELETTE

If sin had a flavor, it would taste like Evie James.

Evie is a sensual, sexy AF woman who loves her indulgences: food and sex . But events—a trio of them, one might say—shook her belief that she deserved a happy ending. Can an unlikely candidate prove to the brazen siren that she deserves it all and give her everything she's wanted?

*Evie is only available as a special occasion book.

Holding on to Day, Entanglement, and Tranquility are all available on Audiobook at the time of publication. Those Who Are Bound will be available on Audiobook in late Spring 2024.

About the Author

Photo credit: In Her Image Photography

Lilly is a Kansas City native who currently resides in sunny California. She has a degree in English (emphasis on literature) from The University of Kansas (and an incomplete degree in medieval history, so does that count? The tuition bills say it does.)

She is a frequent traveler with a soft spot for Ireland, but Puerto Rico is her favorite destination. Alaksa has joined the list of favorites. No matter where she is in the world, however, coffee is a need, necessity, addiction, and obsession (one that she shares with most of her FMCs.)

All of Lilly's books have a playlist on Spotify. Follow the link in her LinkTree: Linktr.ee/LillyKCee

Made in the USA
Columbia, SC
17 November 2024